I0766357

Her DUKE

LUCINDA BRANT BOOKS

— Roxton Foundation Series —
Noble Satyr
His Duchess
Her Duke
Their Graces

— Roxton Family Saga —
Noble Satyr
Midnight Marriage
Autumn Duchess
Dair Devil
Proud Mary
Satyr's Son
Eternally Yours
Forever Remain

— Alec Halsey Mysteries —
Deadly Engagement
Deadly Affair
Deadly Peril
Deadly Kin
Deadly Desire

— Salt Hendon Books —
Salt Bride
Salt Redux

A *New York Times*, *USA Today*, *Amazon*, and *Audible* bestselling author of award-winning Georgian historical romances and mysteries, Lucinda's books are renowned for their wit, heart-felt drama and a happily ever-after. She has degrees in history and political science from the Australian National University and a postgraduate degree in education from Bond University, where she was awarded the Frank Surman Medal. *Noble Satyr*, Lucinda's first novel, was awarded the $10,000 *Random House/-Woman's Day* Romantic Fiction Prize, and she has twice been a finalist for the Romance Writers' of Australia Romantic Book of the Year. Her novels have garnered multiple awards and become worldwide genre bestsellers. Lucinda lives a stone's throw from the beach, in a writing hut with wall-to-wall books on all aspects of the Eighteenth Century, collected over 40 years—Heaven. She loves to hear from readers (and she'll write back!).

lucindabrant@gmail.com	|	lucindabrant.com
pinterest.com/lucindabrant	|	twitter.com/lucindabrant
facebook.com/lucindabrantbooks	|	youtube.com/lucindabrantauthor

Her DUKE

SEQUEL TO HIS DUCHESS

Roxton Foundation Series Book Three

Lucinda Brant

A Sprigleaf Book
Published by Sprigleaf Pty. Ltd.

Her Duke: Sequel to *His Duchess*.
Roxton Foundation Series, Book 3.
Copyright © 2023 Lucinda Brant, all rights reserved.
Editing: Martha Stites & Cathie Maud Cabot.
Art & design: Sprigleaf.
Original artwork reference: *Portrait of Duval de l'Épinoy,
marquis de Saint-Vrain* by Maurice Quentin de La Tour.
Back cover 'postcard' crop art: *A Stag Hunt at Versailles* attributed
to Jean-Baptiste Martin.

Tricorn rider fleuron design by Sprigleaf.

Typeset in Adobe Garamond Pro.

Also in ebook, audiobook, and other languages.

ISBN 978-1-922985-56-9

10 9 8 7 6 5 4 3 2 1 Casebound Library Edition   (ii) I

for
Cathie

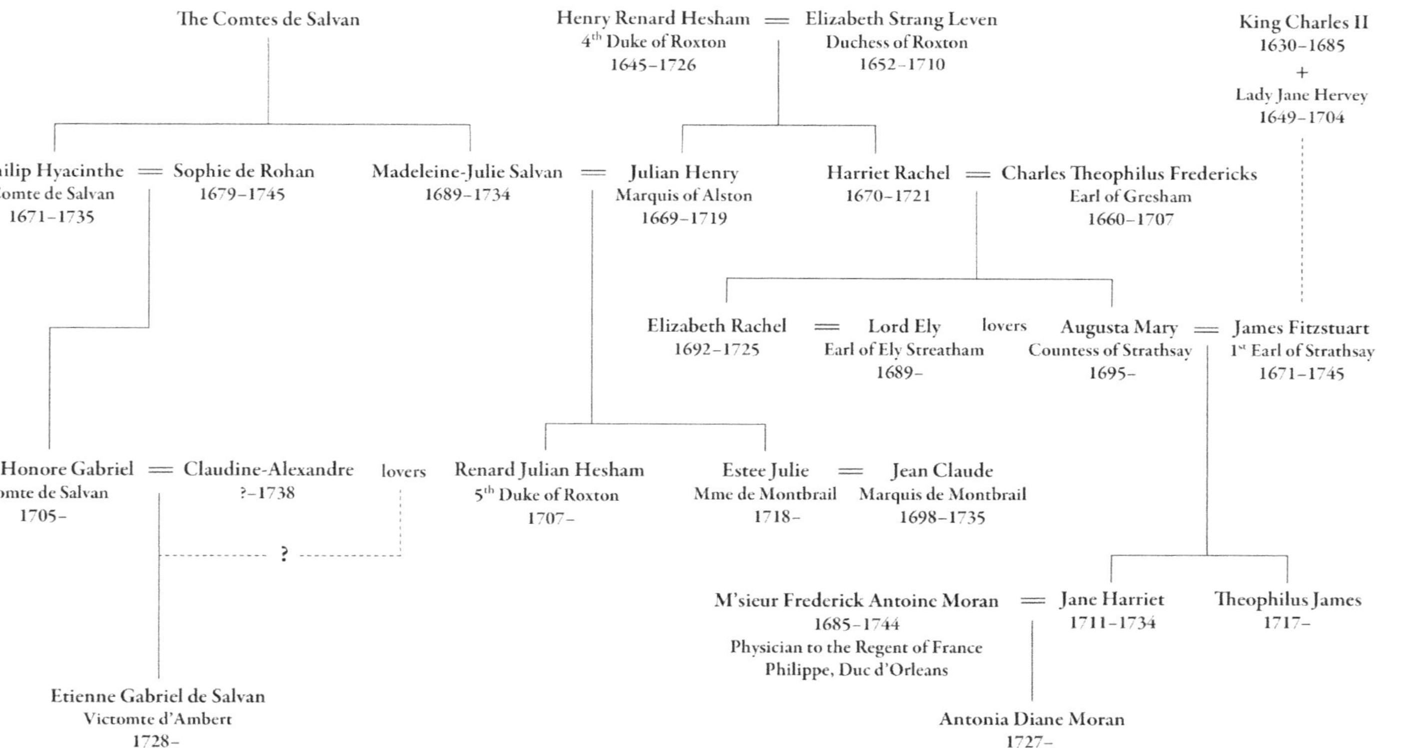

The Comtes de Salvan

Henry Renard Hesham
4th Duke of Roxton
1645–1726
=
Elizabeth Strang Leven
Duchess of Roxton
1652–1710

King Charles II
1630–1685
+
Lady Jane Hervey
1649–1704

Philip Hyacinthe
Comte de Salvan
1671–1735
=
Sophie de Rohan
1679–1745

Madeleine-Julie Salvan
1689–1734
=
Julian Henry
Marquis of Alston
1669–1719

Harriet Rachel
1670–1721
=
Charles Theophilus Fredericks
Earl of Gresham
1660–1707

Elizabeth Rachel
1692–1725
=
Lord Ely
Earl of Ely Streatham
1689–
lovers
Augusta Mary
Countess of Strathsay
1695–
=
James Fitzstuart
1st Earl of Strathsay
1671–1745

Jean-Honore Gabriel
Comte de Salvan
1705–
=
Claudine-Alexandre
?–1738
lovers

Renard Julian Hesham
5th Duke of Roxton
1707–

Estee Julie
Mme de Montbrail
1718–
=
Jean Claude
Marquis de Montbrail
1698–1735

?

M'sieur Frederick Antoine Moran
1685–1744
Physician to the Regent of France
Philippe, Duc d'Orleans
=
Jane Harriet
1711–1734

Theophilus James
1717–

Etienne Gabriel de Salvan
Victomte d'Ambert
1728–

Antonia Diane Moran
1727–

DRAMATIS PERSONAE

The Roxton Family and household

Roxton—*Duke of Roxton aka M'sieur le Duc*

Antonia—*Duchess of Roxton aka Mme la Duchesse
aka Comtesse du Roucy.*

Vallentine—*Lucian, Lord Vallentine, Roxton's best
friend and married to his sister.*

Estée—*Lady Vallentine aka Madame, Vallentine's
wife and Roxton's sister.*

Martin—*Martin Ellicott, Roxton's former valet and
Julian's godfather* (mon parrain).

Julian—*Roxton and Antonia's infant son aka JuJu.*

Gabrielle—*Antonia's personal maid, youngest sister of
Yvette, Rose, and Giselle.*

Céleste & Cécile—*infant Julian's wet nurses aka the
Morvan* nourrices.

George Geraghty—*Roxton's valet.*

Jean-Luc Levron—*natural son of Roxton's father the
Marquis of Alston and his mistress, a* marionnettiste.

Augusta Fitzstuart—*the Countess of Strathsay aka*
Grand-mère. *Antonia's grandmother.*

The Salvan Family and household

The ancient aunts—*sisters of Philip, Comte de Salvan. Roxton's aunts through his mother Madeleine-Julie; Salvan's aunts through his father Philip.*

Tante Philippe—*Marquise du Touraine-Brissac aka Mme Touraine-Brissac. Mother of Alphonse, Duc du Touraine. Grandmother of Elisabeth-Louise and Michelle Haudry.*

Tante Victoire—*the Comtesse du Chavigny.*

Tante Sophie-Adelaide—*twin sister of Victoire. A nun.*

Madeleine-Julie Salvan Hesham—*youngest of the Salvan sisters. Marquise of Alston, Roxton and Estée's mother d. 1734.*

Salvan—*Jean-Honoré Gabriel Salvan, Comte de Salvan. Son of Philip, Comte de Salvan, Roxton's first cousin. Nephew of the ancient aunts.*

Chevalier Montbelliard—*aka Cousin Hugh. The Comte de Salvan's heir.*

Michelle Haudry—*aka Mme Haudry, daughter-in-law of a Farmer General, daughter of Alphonse, Duc du Touraine, granddaughter of Philippe, Marquise du Touraine-Brissac.*

Alphonse—*Duc du Touraine, only son of Mme Touraine-Brissac, Roxton's first cousin and best friend. Father of Michelle Haudry and Elisabeth-Louise Salvan Gondi Touraine.*

Elisabeth-Louise—*sister of Michelle Haudry, granddaughter of Mme Touraine-Brissac.*

Thérèse—*Comtesse Duras-Valfons, Roxton's ex-mistress, wife of Baron Thesiger, sister of the Marquis de Chesnay, mother of the infant Robert.*

Gustave—*Marquis de Chesnay, Roxton's friend, brother of Thérèse Duras-Valfons.*

'Ricky'—*Richard Thesiger, Baron Thesiger, estranged husband of Thérèse Duras-Valfons.*

Giselle—*Elizabeth-Louise's personal maid, sister of Gabrielle.*

Historical figures appearing or mentioned

Louis—*King of France. Louis XV (1710–1774), known as Louis the Well-Beloved, King from 1 September 1715 until his death in 1774.*

Mme de Pompadour—*the King's* maîtresse-en-titre *(official chief mistress) aka Marquise de Pompadour, born Jeanne Antoinette Poisson (1721–1764).*

Comte d'Hozier—*the King's genealogist, keeper of* L'Armorial général de France *and* juge d'armes de France. *Louis Pierre d'Hozier (1685–1767).*

Marquis de Dreux-Brézé—Grand maître des cérémonies de France.

Joachim—*Marquis of Dreux-Brézé (1710-1781)*

Duc de Bouillon—*Grand Chambellan de France.*

Duc de Richelieu—*aka Armand, First Gentleman of the Bedchamber. Louis François Armand de Vignerot du Plessis (1696–1788).*

Marie Leszczyńska—*Queen of France (1703-1768), wife of King Louis XV.*

Marquis de Maurepas—*Minister of the King's Household. Jean-Frédéric Phélypeaux, Count of Maurepas (1701–1781) French statesman.*

M'sieur de Marville—*Lieutenant General of Police for Paris.*

ONE

HÔTEL ROXTON, RUE SAINT-HONORÉ, PARIS, EARLY NOVEMBER 1746.

THE ROTUND imperious porter of the Hôtel Roxton staggered back and bowed so low his nose would have hit his knees had his belly not been in the way. He glimpsed polished leather boots, and the glint of an ornate scabbard amongst the soft folds of a many-caped black roquelaure, as the nobleman crossed the black-and-white marbled tiles of the cavernous entrance foyer.

"M'sieur le Duc! What a—what a-a pl-pl-pleasure to have you home!" he stammered as he straightened. "We—we were not expecting you! What a surprise!"

"That was the point, Christoph," the Duke of Roxton drawled. "To—er—*surprise* you all."

The porter snapped his fingers, and two liveried footmen closed the heavy double fronted doors. Two more of their fellows stepped forward and divested their noble master of felt tricorne, winter cloak, and sword. And when Roxton stripped off his black leather gloves and held them aloft, they were instantly taken by a footman.

He would have continued on, up the wide marble staircase, but a low rumble overhead gave him pause. It was not thunder. It was his army of soft-footed servants jolted into action. The sound never failed to give him a sense of well-being, and it always brought out a thin smile of satisfaction. He did not doubt it was his empty carriage turning in through the main gates that had alerted the household to his arrival.

Earlier, he'd had his driver set him down in the Tuileries gardens, and ordered he wait twenty minutes before continuing on without him, around to the front entrance of his mansion on the Rue Saint-Honoré. Meanwhile, he went for a stroll down the tree-lined avenue and entered his Parisian abode by a side gate. This gate was set in a high wall and gave access to the Tuileries gardens from the bottom of his extensive private garden.

Once inside his dominion, he took a leisurely walk up through the grove of chestnut trees, crossed the ornamental gardens to a colonnade and went under a tall archway that opened out into the expansive entrance courtyard which fronted the street. He arrived at the double front doors to find them bolted and locked against trespass. This pleased him. He used the heavy silver knocker to bang out his arrival.

On his stroll, he was stopped on no fewer than four occasions: By the guards stationed at the side gate, and then by two of their colleagues, part of a small armed force patrolling the inner perimeter of the entire property morning, noon, and night; even one of the sweeps tending to the gravel paths criss-crossing the ornamental gardens boldly waylaid him. Finally, under the colonnade, his head gardener stepped away from a group of men, their heads bent over a set of plans spread out on a trestle table, and demanded that he state his business. As with the guards and the sweep, it took only the lifting of his chin, so his face was no longer obscured by his tricorne, to spark recognition. It was gratifying that every one of his servants registered wide-eyed alarm before instantly dropping their gaze and falling into a silent, respectful bow.

He spent a few moments with his head gardener, perusing the

plans the men were inspecting for the rose hothouses he wanted built within the precinct of the vegetable garden. Pleased at their progress, he left them, making a mental note to commend his steward for keeping his household on the alert to his directive: No one who was not personally known to M'sieur le Duc's immediate family, or had a purpose for being at the hôtel first vetted by the steward, was permitted inside the gates for any reason. The safety and wellbeing of the Duchess and his little lordship were paramount. It mattered not that the Duke and his family were presently residing in the hamlet of Versailles—the directive must be enforced. In this way, with time, it would become second nature, not only to all those in his employ, but also to the members of his extended family.

He was thinking principally of his sister Estée, and her regular open-house *levées* and *soirées* for Parisian Society. Over the years, she had become something of a celebrated hostess for those members of the aristocracy who eschewed the literary salons, finding themselves out of their depth, and thus the topics dull beyond belief. He knew her gatherings were taken up with societal gossip, and mostly about the happenings at court, real or imagined. That he was a close friend of *Sa Majesté*, and Estée condescendingly refused to discuss this friendship with her peers, was reason enough for them to believe that she, too, was also in the King's confidence. She was not. Roxton told her nothing, and she knew not to ask.

And while he had given very little consideration to her Salon or its attendees, now he was married he was more circumspect about the visitors to his home and the company his sister kept. One visitor in particular, a cousin on their maternal side, had become a fixture in her drawing room. By all accounts the Chevalier Montbelliard was a young man of innocuous reputation. But he was heir to the disgraced Comte de Salvan, Roxton's sworn enemy, and that should have been enough for Estée to hold the Chevalier at arm's length. She had not. In fact, he had recently learned she had joined the chorus of their Salvan cousins petitioning the King on Montbelliard's behalf to have the young man received at court.

But his sister's salons and the Chevalier were not the reason he had bestirred himself to leave his duchess and return to Paris for the day.

Estée had written that there was a matter of grave importance, one that would have dire consequences for the family, if he did not deal with it at once. She dare not commit the nature of this matter to paper for fear of her letter ending up in the wrong hands. Her fear was a warning, and not written directly to him but in a letter to her husband. This told him that she had reason to believe her correspondence was being opened and read by M'sieur de Marville, the Lieutenant General of the Paris police.

This did not surprise the Duke. It was an open secret that the French aristocracy who resided in Paris had their correspondence opened and read by the Parisian police. It was the only way Louis had a true indication of what his nobles were thinking and planning. But Roxton was not of the French aristocracy, and if Louis wanted to know what he thought he asked him directly. No. There was something—or someone—else at play here. He presumed his sister knew more than she was letting on in her letter, and so he did not delay, and returned to Paris the very next day.

But once back in the opulent surroundings of his hôtel, he took his time to ascend the stairs to the apartment his sister shared with her husband. He needed a moment to brace himself for an interview he knew from long experience would end with her in histrionics and him at the threshold of his tolerance. He did not hold out much hope that morning-sickness had tempered her emotions. One foot across the threshold of her boudoir and he knew that was too much to ask for.

He found her prostrate amongst the plump silk cushions of her gilded chaise longue, *en déshabillé*. She had an arm across her smooth brow and scrunched in her hand was a lace-bordered handkerchief. Her face was concealed by the tiered lace of the *engageantes* at her elbow, but he doubted she was asleep. But when her maid nervously hissed out that M'sieur le Duc had come and her mistress did not sit up, he preferred to give his sister the benefit of the doubt than think her ill-mannered.

"You said it was a matter of life and—er—death," he said in his silky, slightly sinister voice, peering down at her through his quizzing glass. "And so here I am."

TWO

Behind the veil of lace ruffles, Estée Vallentine's eyes opened wide. She hadn't been expecting her brother, but her husband. She knew the moment the Duke's carriage had pulled in through the gates. Her maids had come rushing to tell her, eyes just as wide, and slightly breathless with nervous anticipation that M'sieur le Duc had come home! But Estée did not believe them. She wasn't to be fooled a second time.

Had they forgotten what had happened just a sennight ago, when the Duke's carriage arrived at the front doors and every servant had gone into a panic? They had roused her from her bed with the news, and she had instantly jumped out of it, thrown on a silk banyan to have her face applied at her dressing table and then arranged herself on her chaise, features schooled in an expression of long suffering, in anticipation of her brother's visit.

But upon that occasion it was not her brother in the carriage but his barbarian of a valet!

Which was why this time she scoffed when told M'sieur le Duc had arrived home. And after the letter she had sent her husband, she was expecting him to return from Versailles, all concern for her welfare. After all, it was his child she was carrying, and it was because of him she had suffered the worst case of morning sickness any pregnant woman in the history of pregnant women had ever had to endure.

Either way, brother or husband, it did not matter. Both deserved to know just how ill and neglected she was. So she left off eating her breakfast and arranged herself on her chaise longue, arm across her brow with eyes closed, an expression of long suffering hidden behind the trail of lace *engageantes*.

Hearing the greeting, there was no mistaking her brother's soft drawl. And while she was bitterly disappointed it was not her husband come rushing to be at her side, she was secretly pleased the Duke had left his villa to pay her a visit. No doubt because of the implied warning in the letter she had sent her husband. This did not stop her being sulky and exploiting her interesting condition, despite knowing the Duke would see through her performance in an instant.

"I am dying, Roxton, and no one cares!" she announced sullenly, making no attempt to sit up to greet him. She took a great shuddering breath. "My husband he has abandoned me. My family they have gone away, leaving me to rattle around in this empty place all alone, and with servants who do not care in the least if I live or die. Why, oh why did you marry me to a man with the feelings of a-a—with no feelings at all! I am so ill I can barely speak!"

The Duke did not to argue with her. "I see that you are," he quipped, looking about for a place to sit. "But perhaps you would feel less ill if you were to finish your splendid breakfast. Particularly that delectable half-eaten croissant. And your chocolate will not be as pleasant drunk cold."

His pointed stare through his quizzing glass was directed at the low table. It groaned under the weight of silver trays and porcelain plates with a fine assortment of fresh pastries, cold meats, and fresh fruits, as well as a silver monogrammed chocolate pot and dish of hot chocolate.

Estée Vallentine pouted and struggled to sit up. She pulled her diaphanous banyan about her shoulders and made motions for her maid to come forward and tidy away the feminine paraphernalia of fabric swatches, spools of fat satin ribbon, and several articles of clothing heaped at one end of the chaise.

"You have had your breakfast?" she asked in a more conciliatory tone.

"I have. But coffee would be welcome."

"Fresh coffee for M'sieur le Duc," Estée demanded of the maid, who now had her arms full. "And tell Jeanne we are not to be disturbed, except for the coffee!"

Roxton gingerly picked up one of the silk cushions by a large tassel and dropped it to the carpet. Flicking out the skirts of his black velvet frock coat, he perched at the end of the chaise and faced his sister. "You wrong your husband. He is staying with us because you told him to go away and—er—stay away."

"I did. But I didn't think he would."

"Then you do not know him as well as you think you do. Lucian does as he is told. And that is what you told him to do."

Estée screwed up her lovely mouth. "Sometimes—no! Not sometimes—*most of the time*—I think he loves *you* more than he does *me*."

The Duke shrugged a shoulder. "Quite possibly. But you can take comfort in the fact that you are the only woman he loves. May I pass you your plate? You will feel better if you eat. Or so your physician advises me."

Estée sat up taller, aghast. "He spies on me to you?"

"No. He informs me as to the wellbeing of my sister. I have a brother's very natural concern for his sister's welfare, particularly in your present condition. And your physician only tells me when I ask."

"How considerate of him!"

"I thought so," he replied nonchalantly, and passed her a Sèvres plate that had upon it a finely sliced pear and a half-eaten croissant. When she hesitated, he added gently, "Please, *ma chère soeur*, you will feel better if you eat."

She nodded, the uncharacteristic kindness in his voice forming a lump in her throat and making her confess, "I find that eating small meals throughout the day has helped stem my nausea."

He watched her pull apart the delicate layers of pastry and consume the rest of the croissant, surprising her with a confession. "Our mother suffered nausea when she was pregnant with you."

"She did? Maman never told me that."

"Nor I. Recently I had a flash of memory of when she was too unwell to rise from her couch. I did not understand at the time. Particularly when *mon père* was overjoyed at her being ill—or so I thought. She scolded him for his happiness. But thinking back on it she was not angry with him. Their behavior confused me greatly. That's when he took me aside and confided I could expect a brother or sister in the new year."

"He wanted another son."

"He did not make his preference known. He was merely happy to be a father again. I, on the other hand, was most annoyed at the prospect of having a sibling and thus a disruption to my life."

"I do not doubt that you did not want a brother or a sister!" Estée replied with a chuckle. "You had been an only child for so long that it must have come as a shock to share our parents with another, and a *bébé*."

"It did," Roxton said seriously. "I am not the sharing type."

"That is not true!" his sister countered vehemently in an about-face. "You are most generous with me and with Lucian, and Antonia you spoil." She finished the slices of pear and put the plate aside with a sidelong glance at the Duke. "And if what I am told is true, you are generous beyond what is tolerable with others who are not even related by blood. *Tante Philippe* told me the most surprising piece of gossip, wanting confirmation. I had not received Lucian's letter then, so it was a simple thing for me to deny it because I was ignorant. But then Lucian's letter arrived, and there it was in ink! Which means I am no longer ignorant, and if asked by our Salvan relatives, I will have to confirm what I know is true. Even so, I cannot believe what you have done! There must be some other explanation."

The Duke was brusque.

"Do me the courtesy of not prevaricating."

She tilted her little nose at him. "Very well. Lucian informed me that you have made that barbarian—your valet—*a mere servant* —a-a gentleman of means!"

"I have."

"With a thousand pounds a year—*for life*."

"That too."

"And you have put a country house at his disposal for a peppercorn rent."

"Yes." The Duke produced his gold and enamel snuffbox from a pocket of his waistcoat. "I trust your husband did not leave off the small detail that along with the yearly income and the country house, there is also a clothing allowance." He smiled thinly. "A gentleman of means must also look the part; do you not agree?"

"A clothing—*clothing allowance*?" Estée gaped at him. "This is —this is—"

"—my business, not yours."

"—*intolerable*." She sniffed her contempt. "I most certainly do not agree! And it *is* my business—*your family's* business. When it becomes common knowledge, we are bound to suffer from-from —*humiliation* at the-the—*scandal* from such an impetuous and-and *ludicrous* undertaking."

"I am never impetuous. And if others think it ludicrous, let them."

"What of the *shame*?"

"Are you referring to the man's morals or his manners? Both are sound, I assure you."

"Roxton! This is not a cavalier matter!"

The Duke tapped the lid of his snuffbox. "No. It is not."

"You cannot have thought through what this means for us," Estée persisted.

She was deaf to the Duke's flat tone and the tapping of his snuffbox which, if she knew her brother half as well as she ought, were sure signs the matter was not open for discussion. But he allowed her some latitude upon this occasion because of her delicate condition, and after taking snuff said with all the patience he could muster,

"If a French king can elevate a bourgeois to *mistress-en-titre* and create her a noblewoman, then there is no cause to make comment when an English duke makes his valet a gentleman of independent means."

Estée knew he was referring to Jeanne-Antoinette Poisson d'Étiolles, wife of a Parisian financier and Louis' official mistress. Louis had raised up Mme d'Étiolles into the nobility as Marquise de Pompadour, and it was a scandal of epic proportions amongst the aristocracy. Tradition dictated the King choose an official mistress from within their ranks. All previous kings had done so, and so had this Louis with the four de Mailly sisters. Which made it all the more incomprehensible why he had not done so again. It was such a contentious appointment that the newly minted Marquise was instantly resented, reviled, and slandered by the people whose ranks she had joined.

If she were thinking rationally, Estée would have seen that it was petty of her to be outraged that her brother had chosen for special favor a man who had given twenty years' loyal service, and who had known the Duke since they were boys.

After all, what was the harm in it? Roxton had always lived as he pleased, and if it pleased him to provide for his valet, then so be it. It would hardly impact upon her life. Or so she had at first thought until her Salvan aunts—her mother's sisters, and from an old French aristocratic family—expressed their outrage, convincing her otherwise.

Whoever heard of a lackey being singled out in such a peculiar way? Not they! Rarely were servants paid on time, some not at all if they were recalcitrant. It was a privilege for the lower orders to serve their noble masters. Any remuneration was secondary to this service. And as this flunkey had accepted such an outrageous offer from his master, he was obviously a mercenary who cared more about pecuniary gain than the honor done him being a duke's valet. The honorable course of action was to refuse and look forward to a small bequest upon his master's death. That was the right way to go about such matters. Anything else had the odor of the bourgeoisie about it. This servant was just as coarse a personage as that fishwife who was *Sa Majesté's* whore!

The ancient aunts worried for M'sieur le Duc d'Roxton's sanity. To create his valet a gentleman of independent means was not only unconscionable it was the stuff of lunacy. What flea had entered her brother's ear?

Estée tearfully recounted all this to her stony-faced brother.

How the delegation of their ancient aunts called upon her and told her of the whispers of M'sieur le Duc's shocking and frivolous whim concerning his servant that was presently circulating the salons of their friends and relations, the alcoves of gaming clubs, even the high-class brothels frequented by noblemen. The ancient aunts said the family had suffered enough humiliation with its head, the Comte de Salvan banished from court, and that had been at the hands of M'sieur le Duc d'Roxton. And now this latest peculiar behavior of their nephew had everyone questioning the efficacy of the Salvan bloodline. That perhaps the family was cursed. Who would want to align themselves and marry their son or daughter into a family where one nephew had been banished from court, and the other was frittering away his wealth on a menial? It was humiliation piled upon humiliation.

And after the interrogation she'd received from *Tante Philippe,* the most formidable of the ancient aunts, Estée had been left so fatigued she'd taken to her bed for days! She wondered if her baby would be affected by her melancholy. And this despite the ancient aunts reassuring her it was not her fault, and they were not angry with her. They knew precisely where to lay the blame, and what flea had got into their nephew's ear for him to enact such a ridiculous flight of fancy. It was the same flea that had infected their other nephew the Comte de Salvan to act the madman.

And when they told her the flea's name, Estée was not at all surprised. It was the only plausible explanation. She repeated their accusation now, flinging it at the Duke with all the haughty contempt worthy of her ancient aristocratic Salvan blood.

"You would never have entertained such an absurd notion before your marriage. And that barbarian he would still be your valet and in his proper place, and we and our Salvan relatives would not now be considered the nincompoops of the world, if not for her! This—this—*catastrophe*—it is all Antonia's doing!"

THREE

Tʜᴇ Dᴜᴋᴇ's usual characteristic response to his sister's tearful petulant outbursts was to set his jaw and remain impassive, then await one of two outcomes: Emotionally exhausted and free of tears she would come to her senses but remain sullen; or she would throw herself amongst the cushions, beyond rational conversation. Either way he got the same result: her silence. This would then allow him to issue his directive then depart as swiftly as possible, and often to the accompaniment of sobs and the hushed platitudes of comfort offered to her by her women. This had been the way of things between brother and sister since he had come into the title almost twenty years ago.

This time his response was different. Why it was different was because of a remark his duchess had made the night before, when he had told her he was required to return to Paris for the day to reluctantly deal in person with a matter concerning his sister and the ancient aunts. He said he would do his best to be particularly sensitive to Estée's needs given her pregnancy and morning sickness, but that he did not hold out any hope of there not being a dramatic scene involving tears and accusations of ill treatment.

Antonia had remarked that she was not at all surprised that this would be Estée's response, and neither should he be because his sister had been raised in a house of tears.

The Duke was puzzled. "House of tears, *ma vie?*"

"The hôtel, when your mother and sister they lived there alone without you," Antonia explained matter-of-factly. And when he continued to look none the wiser, she added as if it was self-evident, "But it must have been a house of tears, Monseigneur. Your father he died suddenly, leaving a young widow with a small son and a *bébé*. And then only a few months later, you—your mother's only son and now head of the family—were forcibly removed from her care by your grandfather, never to be seen again for many years. So your mother she suffered all over again with this second bereavement at your loss.

"Your sister she was just an infant at the time, so she never knew her papa, and while she was told she had a brother, you did not come into her life until she was well into her girlhood, so you were no more than a phantom. And so she would never have known a time when her maman she was happy. Your maman she remained in mourning the rest of her life, always sad and always close to tears. Her women and their servants they would have been greatly affected by such unhappiness. How then could the hôtel be a home when it was a house of tears? Any little girl—all children— deserve to be surrounded by happiness and light. But Estée she was not. And so she responds in the only way she knows how, with tears."

Antonia had then kissed his cheek at what must have been a sudden spark of realization in his eyes, adding with a dazzling smile, "But now we have Julian, and Lucian and Estée are soon to have their own *bébé*, the house of tears must become for all a distant memory, yes? The hôtel is to be a happy home for our children, and for all of us. We must make it so."

The Duke agreed. Further pondering Antonia's acute observation on the carriage ride to Paris, he thought it true in every particular. Thus when his sister burst into tears after she had sullenly thrown her accusation about the Duchess at his head, instead of issuing his directive and taking his leave, he bit down on his response and remained perched on the chaise longue.

Taking a deep mental breath, he handed Estée his clean white linen handkerchief, saying gently, "Dry your eyes, *ma chère soeur*, and we will talk…Ah! And here is the coffee."

One of Estée Vallentine's women had tiptoed into the room carrying a tray of coffee things in her shaking hands. The Duke directed she put the tray on the low table and take her leave. He would make his own coffee. Not a glance at her mistress, she scurried away, leaving the siblings alone in an uncharacteristically and eerily silent boudoir.

THE DUKE MADE coffee for them both, while Estée dabbed at her eyes and delicately patted her face dry. She sat with his handkerchief scrunched in her silken lap, a wary eye on her brother after her outburst. But when he handed her a porcelain dish with coffee made the way she preferred, and sat sipping from his dish in silence, she relaxed. He waited until he saw the tension ease in her shoulders, and setting his porcelain dish on its saucer, he explained.

"You are correct on three counts. One: The Duchess has opened my eyes to the effect the—er—extraordinary circumstances of my upbringing has had on my—how do I put it?— unique? Ah! Yes!—*unique* outlook on life. Two: Had I not wed Antonia, there is no doubt Martin would have continued on in his role of valet until one of us met our demise." His smile was self-deprecating. "It seems that neither of us can do without the other… And thirdly: It is because of Antonia that Martin is no longer a servant but a gentleman of independent means. But—"

"I *knew* it had to be her idea!"

"*But*," he enunciated, "it is not the catastrophe you think it, whatever our ancient aunts have been drumming in your little ear to the contrary."

She pouted at the mention of their aunts.

"I do not know how you cannot think it a catastrophe," she grumbled, "when this whim of hers will cost you the better part of forty thousand pounds. And that is if you are unlucky enough that he has the good fortune not to be struck down by any number of ills before he reaches old age!"

The Duke gave a low chuckle.

"What mental ruminations you and our aunts get up to over the chocolate pot! Or should that be cauldron…? If Martin lives well into his seventies, then the amount will be closer to fifty thousand, if one takes into account the house put at his disposal, and the clothing allowance."

"*Mon Dieu*," Estée muttered as she set her dish on its saucer. "Think what better use you could have made of such a fortune, and you are wasting it on a menial!"

"I do not doubt that too was precisely the response of our avaricious aunts," Roxton quipped. He frowned and let out a small breath. "I am not surprised by their reaction, but I am disappointed that *you* would parrot them."

His gaze flickered about the ostentatious room with its silk floral wallpaper, gilded and velvet upholstered furniture, deep carpets, and the hundred-and-one expensive feminine trinkets in porcelain, crystal, and luxurious textiles his sister considered necessary for her comfort, none of which were to his taste and made the space feel nauseatingly cramped.

He added on a light, ironic note, "If you have a genuine complaint about the style and level of comfort I waste on you, then please, here is your opportunity to voice your dissatisfaction and request further remuneration."

"Waste?" Estée blinked at him in astonishment and sat up tall. "You compare me, *your sister*—whose bloodline is not only of the

English nobility but also of the French *noblesse d'épée*—with your *valet*, a-a mere lackey who—"

"Have you ever calculated the amount I expend yearly on your wants and needs?"

"Why would I do such a needless thing?" Estée wondered, baffled. "Expenses are necessary if we are to live as our noble blood demands. To do anything less would be to dishonor our name and our ancestors. And it would be a dishonor to you, not only as head of our family, but as the most powerful duke in England, for me to present to the world as anything less than I do. I am your sister. *Enfin.*"

Roxton inclined his head in acceptance of this.

"Yet, I suspect the majority of our noble brethren on this side of the Channel have never tallied the expenses they incur to do their noble lineage justice. They live well beyond their means, trumpeting a way of life they can ill afford, but which they demand of each other. And they will keep up this pretence until their last breath, with no thought to ever settling their considerable debts, the burden then left to their children, and their children's children, to shoulder."

"What a thoroughly miserable picture you paint of our French friends and relations!" She peered at him with genuine puzzlement and was suddenly alarmed. "Are you trying to tell me I must economize?"

He gave an involuntary bark of laughter.

"God forbid any member of my family must needs pull in the purse strings!" he remarked, tongue-in-cheek. "Fear not," he added with a supercilious smile. "I am wealthier today than I was yesterday. My children will have no debts, and considerably more than the vast fortune I inherited on the demise of the fourth duke."

Estée sighed her relief "I am glad to hear it." She gave an unladylike snort of dismissal. "But please do not make a habit of gifting your riches to menials, or the tide might turn on your wealth!"

"Dear me. The ancient aunts have laid siege to your better nature, haven't they?" the Duke drawled with one brow raised in disapproval. "Be assured that if you live four score years, your clothing allowance alone will have drained my coffers in excess of a hundred thousand pounds."

Estée could not hide the surprise in the widening of her blue eyes, but she dissembled, putting up her little nose as if this was nothing new to her. "My gown allowance is a paltry two thousand pounds per annum—"

"Do the math, Estée."

"I refuse! That would be vulgar."

He held her gaze without a smile. "As vulgar as discussing my wealth with our ancient aunts."

Her face fired red with embarrassment because she could not deny it, but she did her best to make amends, laying a hand on his upturned velvet cuff.

"You do know how eternally grateful I am—we both are—for everything you do for me and for Lucian. I am not as ignorant as you suppose. I know we could not live as we do if not for your generosity. But—Roxton! I am your *sister*, and Lucian he is your brother-in-law; we are *family*. Why, even our mother's sisters are family and deserving of your consideration before that barbarian. He has not one drop of our noble blood, nor can he own to a lineage worthy of your—"

"His name is Martin Ellicott, and you will do him and me the courtesy of calling him by his name—Martin or Ellicott—either one will suffice, although—" Roxton put up a long finger and thought a moment. "I think it best that you ask him which he prefers when next he is seated across from you—"

"*Seated?*" She was horrified. "*In my presence?*"

"—as he will be, at table, given he is now part of *my* family. That entitles him to live under my roof, eat at my table, and partake of my company, whenever it suits *him*. And he will sit where he pleases. You, and our mother's sisters, will treat him with the respect deserving of a most trusted friend of M'sieur le Duc d'Roxton, or there will be—er—consequences."

Estée stared at him with mouth open and dared to huff her incredulity. "*Consequences*? Throwing away a fortune on a menial is outrageous enough, but making him part of our family—"

"I have."

"—will be seen as an affront to our dignity by-by—oh! By *everyone*!"

"I have not the least interest in how *everyone* views the matter. All I require is silent acceptance."

"You are only doing this because Antonia wishes it!"

"We both wish it."

She looked at him askance and needlessly smoothed a hand across her satin quilted petticoat. "And if I do not feel *inclined* to allow him to sit in my presence, or want to discover which name he prefers…?"

He smiled crookedly. "Ah, and I thought you quicker of brain than that. But let me spell it out for you, lest your pregnancy has dulled your senses. I am not making a request, but an edict. I am expecting you to act in a particular way. If you do not…?" He pulled a face. "I would hate for you to struggle into last season's gowns to attend the Opera and the little parties of your friends, particularly in your growing condition."

Estée drew in a breath, mortified. "You—you would limit my allowance, all because I deem it inappropriate for one of my lineage to share a meal with one who has no lineage at all—"

"He's not contagious, Estée."

"He might very well be for the purposes of upholding our nobility! And when Society learns I am breaking bread with one who should be below stairs making the bread? I will be the scoffing-stock of Paris! And our family will be the butt of cruel jokes!" She dabbed at her moist eyes and sniffed. "You cannot make me! *You* can weather such taunts—no one would dare say a word to you, and you do not care for people's opinions—but I cannot. And

I do care what is said about me and about our family—*very much*. And in my present delicate condition, I fear I do not have the strength to weather such *humiliation*. What do I tell our aunts? What will our Salvan cousins think? How will I *ever* face them with my chin up if you make me do this?"

Roxton resisted the urge to roll his eyes and counted to five. He reminded himself of the house of tears, and kept his annoyance in check.

"As my sister you can and you will get through this," he stated firmly. "When out in Society all you need do is remember that your brother is the wealthiest noble either side of the Channel. That while you wear jewels those around you wear paste, not because they fear highwaymen—whatever they say to the contrary —but because the jewels they inherited from their ancestors were pawned many moons ago. No doubt sold to Farmers-General for the swan-like necks of their common-born mistresses. Do as you always have done—shrug your lovely shoulder and brush aside any matter you find unsavory." He smiled crookedly. "You've had plenty of practice in the past when questioned about my—er —*nefarious* activities. As for our ancient aunts, I will deal with our mother's sisters." He lost his smile and put up his brows. "Need I concern myself as to whom my sister owes her loyalty?"

She was offended. "Of course not! And you need never ask!" But she could not help throwing out at him sullenly, "Ellicott must mean a great deal to you."

"He does, to both of us. A thousand pounds a year is small compensation for a lifetime of love and devotion. No amount of money can buy *that*. And lest you worry Martin's allowance will impinge on you continuing to live in the style to which you are deserving, let me ease your mind. His allowance comes not from my coffers, but from the inheritance Antonia was bequeathed by her grandfather."

"But when she married you, what was hers became yours, to do with as you please."

The Duke inclined his head at the universal truth of this. "Yet I would never deny her. She asked that I honor her birthday by using a third of her grandfather's inheritance to provide Martin with an independent living. The rest will be put in trust for Julian to access after his twenty-first birthday."

Estée gaped at him. "The Earl of Strathsay bequeathed Antonia one hundred and fifty thousand pounds?"

"You *are* capable of mental arithmetic! Bravo."

"Is there any wonder why Salvan schemed to marry her! Such a fortune would have solved all his monetary woes—"

"—and the pecuniary problems of our ancient aunts and their offspring," the Duke drawled with a sneer. "Although I do not now believe the General Earl's fortune was the singular object of why Salvan tried to force a match with Antonia. Do not misconstrue me. Salvan wanted Antonia, and he wanted her fortune, and so did our aunts. But their eyes were on a bigger prize, and *that* was inherited through her father."

"I do not understand. Antonia's father was penniless at his death. Or that was what we believed to be true"

"He was."

"Then what was in his possession that could possibly be worth more than an inheritance of a hundred and fifty thousand pounds?"

"All in good time, my dear." The Duke patted her hand, then stood to stretch his legs. "I must thank you and Lucian again for lugging back from Italy Antonia's trunk of childhood possessions. As you know, her father's will was amongst those belongings, and it proved most illuminating. He had in fact spent his fortune on establishing a small hospital for indigent females, particularly those who were unmarried and with child. Upon his death he left what coin he had, and his house, for the hospital's upkeep."

"*Mon Dieu.* To not provide for his only child is unconscionable!"

"I do believe money for its own sake held very little value for him," the Duke mused. "Which, when one thinks about it, is precisely what one would expect from an eccentric and brilliant physician who devoted his life to tending the poor and wretched, but who was also a nobleman of the *noblesse d'épée*."

"How proud he would be of his daughter," she retorted. "It seems that Antonia not only inherited her father's intelligence and eccentricity but also his lack of concern for keeping wealth within the family. *Seigneur*! He ignored her needs, frittering away what little he had on those who were least deserving of it."

Roxton startled her by grinning.

"Spoken like a true Salvan." But his smile vanished just as quickly as it had appeared, and he sighed his disappointment at her lack of understanding. "I should not be surprised," he muttered. "If one spends enough time around vultures one starts to smell like carrion…"

It was an oblique reference to her childhood in the stultifying company of their cheerless Salvan aunts, and a mother who remained in a perpetual state of mourning. And while he was prepared to excuse much of her behavior on this saturnine upbringing, when she went that one step too far—pouring oil on the simmering flame of his tolerance by daring to malign his duchess—there was an end to his patience.

"You think me hard-hearted, but I tell you this in your best interests," she stated primly, encouraged by his uncharacteristic benevolence in listening to her complaints to voice what she had only ever dared to whisper with her aunts. "If you do not restrain Antonia she will become ungovernable. She has already caused consternation and disruption below stairs with the unnecessary introduction of a plethora of provincial servants. As I said to her: It is one thing to employ Morvan *nourrice*s to feed your infant, quite another to allow them to bring their families into the household. It is beyond what is acceptable. You have been driven out of this house and into a villa all to please her! And now there is this latest whim—throwing away her inheritance on a lackey."

She scoffed and continued, barely drawing breath.

"One wonders what excesses tomorrow will bring. You reassure me we have no monetary concerns but as surely as the sun sets in the evening, if you do not put a stop to her—to her—*charitable dissipation*, it will be *your* wealth she'll be squandering next. Before you know it—" She snapped her fingers. "—we will be forced to be just as niggardly as our ancient aunts!"

"Enough."

"You glare at me as if I have two heads, but we—our mother's sisters and I—we are all in agreement that you over-indulge your wife—" When the Duke stepped up to her chaise, he stood so close she had to fall back amongst the cushions to look up at him. What she saw reflected in his black eyes had her catching her breath in astonishment. "You—you are angry with *me* for voicing what we all know to be—to be the-the—*truth*?"

"That remarkably witless diatribe was unworthy even of you," he said in a voice so quiet she had to strain to hear him. But there was no mistaking his arctic fury. "Those who do not know Antonia want to believe the slanderous whispers doing the rounds of the salons—that her great beauty and sanguine disposition go hand-in-hand with a dim-witted and vapid intelligence. Those same dolts dare to repeat degrading calumnies such as I have allowed unbridled lust for exquisite beauty to bewitch me into acting foolishly out of character. That I have thrown to the four winds my good sense, wealth, honor, and everything and anything else they can think of to slur our good name, and I have done so all to indulge my wife? They want to see me brought to my knees. But you—*my sister*—know us both better than anyone alive. So for you to *dare* question my intelligence—worse!—denigrate *her*—she who has only brought joy and love into our lives—not only offends me, but it belittles *you*. Be warned, Estée: The bond that binds us as brother and sister could not be stretched any thinner, were it to snap here and now!

"But I will excuse and forget your sanctimonious flummery

upon this occasion because of your delicate condition," he continued in a more even tone. "And because it is obvious you have been left alone in this house far too long, so that your mind has festered as a result, it is as well I brought the large carriage to convey you to the villa. A few days of country air before Antonia's presentation will revive your good sense. Now let us have a fresh pot of coffee and discuss what it is you could not put in a letter. Your husband tells me—"

Unable to control herself a moment longer, Estée burst into sobs and threw herself face down into her silk cushions.

The Duke rolled his eyes heavenward, locked his jaw and retreated to the window to stare unseeing at the view. His assurances and good intentions of his visit not ending with his sister in tears were in tatters.

FOUR

Estée's sobs brought her women, flinging aside the tapestry *portière* to rush into the boudoir, wide-eyed and anxious. They stopped all at once, tripping over each other upon seeing the Duke. They had been confident he must have taken his leave, as he always did when their mistress burst into tears, leaving them to coax her down from a high passion. They would not have entered the boudoir otherwise. But as M'sieur le Duc was still there they did not know what they should do. It was only when he waved a languid hand in acknowledgment of their existence and signalled for them to come into the room that they thawed and quickly went about their business.

He stayed by the undraped window, aquiline profile in silhouette, and patiently waited while his sister was cajoled and fussed over. And while he waited the view of the inner courtyard dissolved, replaced by fragments of memories in his mind's eye.

These memories had been locked away and buried deep within him since his forceable removal from his mother's arms—kidnapped by agents of his English grandfather the fourth duke—when he was not quite twelve years old. He did not return to

France for eight long years. Eight years that were to him a lifetime. He had no contact with his mother, knowing whether she lived or died, and this hôtel which had been his home, where he was born and spent a happy childhood with both his parents, became a distant memory. As for his sister, she was an infant when he was taken and upon his return was a shy little girl who hid behind her nurse's skirts and was afraid of him, a stranger.

And he was a stranger, to her, to his mother, and to himself. He left France a terrified boy and returned a supercilious young man of twenty, the wealthiest nobleman in England, a duke, and head of his family. But he did not return as a son or as a brother. Any familial bond had been beaten or starved out of him by his grandfather. To survive such an ordeal, he had purposely frozen his heart against regret and disappointment, fearing he'd never see his mother again. Then, after one particularly brutal beating for continuing to speak the language of his French forebears, he decided he did not need a heart at all.

Upon his grandfather's death and inheriting the title, he was free to return to France. Which he did. He now realised in leaving England and returning to France, he had left his heart behind, long forgotten that he did not know where to find it and did not think it necessary. And being heartless helped with a family reunion that was, for his mother at least, as emotionally fraught as had been his kidnapping.

For him she was not the mother of his boyhood memories, a loving happy creature who had smothered him in kisses and cuddles and was forever telling him that she loved him. Reunited, she could barely look at him without bursting into tears because he had grown into the image of his father—the husband she had tragically lost. She wore black from head to toe, and was in a state of perpetual mourning. And having returned to the faith of her girlhood before her marriage, she spent her days in prayer, surrounded by nuns and her elderly widowed relatives. She was lost to him. And as his sister had been placed in the *Abbaye-aux-*

Bois—the convent for the daughters of French aristocrats, and there to remain for the next several years—she was lost to him too. Thus it was an easy decision for him to continue on his journey into Italy with Lucian Vallentine.

He could not depart the hôtel quick enough, and had left with a sense of relief mixed with fury—relief to quit an atmosphere of cloying piety, and fury because his grandfather had triumphed. He had detached his grandson from his French parent; fashioned him into the epitome of the haughty English nobleman and, for all intents and purposes, removed his beating heart, for he was surely devoid of all natural feeling. He might be the image of his father, but in every other respect he was his grandfather.

For the longest time he believed this to be true. He also believed there was nothing he could do to change this creature of his grandfather's making—or so he had thought…

And then Antonia had twirled into his life. This vortex of love and light turned his well-ordered world upside down. She said it was not so much that he was heart-*less*, but that he had misplaced it, and she knew where to find it. Not only that, but she would restore it to him and also to his family.

Her emphatic and unswerving belief in him left him dazed, and he was in awe of her *joie de vivre*. And to his astonishment he believed her. Which was just as well, she teased, because her father had told her that what was most important in this life was being loved, being with family, and being true to oneself. He now believed that too.

But while he was prepared to live by these maxims with Antonia, there was one area where he remained unequivocally his grandfather's heir. As Duke of Roxton he commanded and expected absolute loyalty, from every quarter—from family members on down to the scullery maids in his kitchens. Loyalty was rewarded with his munificence and his protection. Those deemed by him to be untrustworthy and undeserving—and that included members of his own family—were ruthlessly discarded.

He was uncompromising and unapologetic, and, he thought with a wry smile, true to himself.

WHEN SUFFICIENTLY IN control of her emotions to sit up and dry her eyes, Estée announced the need to use her porcelain bourdaloue, and with one of her maids disappeared behind the tapestry screen in the far corner of the room. When she emerged, she sat at her dressing table to have face powder reapplied, while two of her women retied the silk ribbons in her black curls. With her banyan straightened over her jumps and quilted petticoats, she sipped at a tumbler of cordial, prescribed by her physician for when she was feeling unwell. And while she sipped, elbows propped on the table and eyes closed, one of her women fanned air across her bosom, another fussed with the pillows on the chaise, and a third directed two maids to clear away the breakfast things.

Her women said not a word, everything communicated with side-long looks and gestures. All were expert in knowing what was required after one their mistress's emotional outbursts. And until she had recovered her sense of well-being, opened her eyes, and spoke first, they mutely carried on with their tasks.

What they were not used to, and what had them on edge was the continued presence of the Duke. It set them all aflutter. So much so that one of them fumbled with the stopper of a crystal jar and it fell with a thud amongst the clutter on the dressing table.

The sudden noise opened Estée's eyes and her mouth, and she was about to chastise the woman's clumsiness when she caught the unfamiliar in the looking glass. Staring past her own reflection and into the room she saw her brother in profile, gazing out the window. It gave her such a jolt that she had to look over her shoulder to make certain the reflection had not deceived her.

It had not. He was still there.

She turned back to the looking glass and stared at her reflection without seeing it. And while it unnerved her he had not taken his leave the moment she burst into tears, she was pleased he had seen for himself what his arguing with her did to her finer feelings. Not for the first, or the hundredth, time did she wonder why it was that whenever they quarrelled, she fell all to pieces and he never did. She would sob her heart out and when emotionally spent lie for hours on her chaise castigating herself for allowing her heart to rule her head, certain her brother had no heart at all.

Her husband said there was no point ruminating and getting herself even more upset, particularly about the unalterable. Her tears and her worry were for naught. And no matter how many tumblers she filled, or silk cushions she ruined with her tears, the incontestable fact was—bruised feelings aside—she owed Roxton her allegiance and obedience. After all, he was her brother and head of the family, and he was also a duke, and not just any duke but the premier duke amongst his peers. Which meant not only was his word law, there really was no other word but his, and he would always have the last word, too. That was just a fact of life.

So unless she wanted to sail off to the Americas and live amongst savages, then she best do as she was told. He did. Life was uncomplicated that way, and pleasant. He didn't care to argue with anyone, and most certainly not with Roxton. He did what and when he was told, and that was that. He left the thinking and the ruminating and the worrying to her brother, and she should too. Oh, and before she made plans to set sail, she should know Roxton would find her wherever she went, and have her dragged back home. He was certain the Duke would not want his sister living with savages.

Besides, he didn't want to live in the New World, he liked the old. And if she left him, he'd be distraught for days. *Days?* She had been instantly incensed, and he quickly corrected himself and said weeks, followed by years; and finally, and only after he covered her face with kisses and admitted he would never make a recover, was she happy and satisfied.

She wished Lucian were there now, to comfort her and kiss her, and tell her she was the most beautiful creature alive.

And while she wanted nothing better than to lie on her chaise and be left alone with her thoughts, she recognised here was a unique situation. For her brother to remain behind after one of her tearful upheavals could only mean that he had more to say to her. Although, when she thought about it, she realised she had yet to divulge to him the most disturbing piece of gossip she had learned from their ancient aunts. And perhaps that was why he remained.

Regardless, she knew it behoved her to set aside her *bruised feelings* and strive to remember that while he was her brother, being sister of a duke was a source of great pride to her, providing her with enviable and unrivalled cachet in Parisian society. And he was not just any duke. To everyone, including himself, he was first, last, and always M'sieur le Duc d'Roxton.

FIVE

W HEN Estée returned to the chaise longue, Roxton left the window and crossed back to where she sat. They were once again alone, her women dismissed to the other side of the *portière*.

She dared to glance up at him but remained demure, hands in her lap. The only sign of any continued agitation was her fiddling with the closed sticks of her fan.

"Are you feeling better for the cordial?" he asked lightly. When she merely nodded, he added in a conciliatory tone, "Forgive me if you thought me harsh. But I am rather sensitive to hearing my duchess aspersed."

"You have a right to your sensitivity." She heaved a sigh of grudging acceptance. "I am the one who must needs ask your forgiveness. Antonia is the sweetest dearest creature alive and the best sister I could ever wish for. And you are the best of brothers," she added in a small voice and took a few shuddering breaths. She glanced up at him again, color in her cheeks. "I-I do not know what came over me to question you, and I apologise. Naturally you are at liberty to do as you wish, as is Antonia. And as your sister I will do whatever it is you require of me where Ellicott is concerned. It may take me some little while to-to *adjust* and-and *remember* that he is now part of the family, but I will try my best."

"Thank you. That is all I ask."

She nodded and sighed heavily. "This wretched pregnancy has surely scrambled *my* good sense!"

"Wretched spiteful ancient aunts more belike," the Duke muttered, still annoyed with himself for allowing his Salvan relatives to get under his skin. "I may not have spelled it out in so many words," he added evenly, "but let me do that for you now, so there is no further need. Antonia does indeed hold great sway over my opinions and actions. That is because she has my best interests at heart, and acts wholly from a position of unconditional love and fierce devotion. She is also wise beyond her years." He smiled self-consciously. "Which is why I will always trust my wife above and before all others."

"I have never thought otherwise," Estée replied without hesitation. "She is your most passionate champion and she loves you unreservedly. As you do her. I am very happy for you both, but—but your marriage it is not what is usual amongst our kind. Which makes me worry for you, and for her, that because you love each other a little too well—"

"—the slanders that swirl around us will inflict an even deeper hurt?" cut in the Duke, to complete her sentence. "But most particularly the hurt will be on her."

"Antonia is unspoilt and I sincerely hope she remains unaffected," she said quietly, and strove to calmly articulate her troubled thoughts. "I know you will do your utmost to see that she is always protected but—Roxton! We inhabit a world that can be cruel and vindictive and unforgiving to those who are not born to it, or who dare to upset the natural order of our way of life. And I do not discount our Salvan relatives from amongst that number. You are right. Our ancient aunts are wretched and spiteful. Antonia has gained their ire because they blame her for Cousin

Salvan's banishment and the loss of his court preferments, and our aunts have suffered financial hardship as a result. They relied on his largesse to upkeep their dignity. Worse still, as a result of his ridiculous scheming to marry Antonia the Salvan name has become synonymous with foolish pride. This has made our ancient aunts not only figures of pity but of gossip, and that they cannot abide. They are very proud vain creatures who were used to being the center of court life and its intrigues. Gone are those days when a Salvan at court was respected, even revered as their brother was revered when he was Comte. It truly is a sad state of affairs for them."

"All of that I know," the Duke stated with indifference. "None of that concerns me. Salvan deserved his punishment, and for their encouragement of his schemes, so do they."

"But for those of our Salvan cousins who were not involved but dragged into the blizzard of Salvan's scheming—such as the Chevalier Montbelliard? Does he deserve to be punished? None of this was of his making."

Roxton thought of the Chevalier's visit to the villa seeking an audience with his Duchess, and upon another occasion, barging into his library with a gift for her birthday supposedly from one of the ancient aunts, but he had his doubts about that, and about the young man in general. There was something about him that would not wash… He roused himself from his thoughts to say flatly,

"I am yet to make a determination of where the Chevalier fits —unwitting schemer, wary adversary, or clueless cub."

"For what my opinion is worth, Montbelliard seems what he appears, a most sincere young man without a deceitful bone in his body."

"Thank you for your opinion. I do not discount it. And if what you say is true, I will not hinder his path to court and the preferments that are to be his when he comes into the title."

"But—it could be years—*decades*—before our Cousin Salvan's demise!"

"Yes."

"Without your support the Chevalier has little hope of being accepted at court. *Sa Majesté* certainly won't entertain his presence without your say-so."

"It is a quandary for the Chevalier to be sure."

The flat note to his voice told her not to continue down that path of discussion. Instead, she took another deep breath and looked up from the closed sticks of her fan to hold her brother's gaze once again.

"You will think me belabouring the point but when it becomes known you have dared to lift a menial up out of servitude at Antonia's behest, not only will our ancient aunts take umbrage, but so will everyone else. There will be a great outcry—"

"I appreciate your concern and you can be assured I am doing all in my power to shield Antonia from the more sordid and spiteful attacks that will be directed her way. Should anyone dare to go so far as to publicly besmirch her, they will be brought swiftly to account."

"Mayhap I am being needlessly anxious on her behalf, but I tell you all of this, not only out of a sense of duty but because I do love you—I love you both. Which makes me worry for you, but mostly for her. That she has blessed you with a son in the first year of your marriage has kept her preoccupied and away from Society, which is not such a bad thing. But now that you mean to have her presented at court, it will require her leaving her gilded cage—"

"Gilded—er—cage?

Estée plucked at the quilting of her silken petticoat. "What *Tante Philippe* calls your little villa at Versailles."

"No guesses that Antonia is the delightful songbird in that cage!" The Duke sneered. "How spitefully apt!"

"But—it is not so far from the truth, is it? You seek to keep her protected, just as one does a songbird, from the cats' claws," his sister argued. "But away from your villa and at court, Antonia will no longer have that protection. You kept me from court because you said a nest of vipers was no place for a young woman of virtue. So I do not understand why you would send your duchess into that very same nest. The ancient aunts think you are doing so as part of a greater game to have your revenge on Salvan—"

"Of course they would," he interrupted tersely. "But this is no game, and Antonia is not a credulous pawn in some scheme of my making. She understands that to accompany me to Louis's little suppers, she must first undergo the very public ordeal of a court presentation. And that is all Society need know."

"There is more you are not telling me."

"There is. Suffice that Antonia is well aware that to ensure the continued happiness of our family, a very public announcement is required."

"It is the public nature of her presentation that has me worried. Naturally no one would dare lay a finger on your duchess. But there is harm of a different kind—the kind that eventuates from public ridicule. And everyone knows how *Sa Majesté* hates to be embarrassed in any way. So if someone were to create a spectacle with the aim of embarrassing Antonia, that would be grounds for Louis to have them banished, yes?"

The Duke raised an eyebrow, intrigued. "Without doubt. You see me suitably baffled, so please do not dither further."

Estée dared to scoff, the words out of her mouth before she had time to think. "There must be any number of persons who wish you harm because of your nefarious misdeeds before marriage!"

"And what would my virtuous sister know of that?"

"I know nothing! Nor do I care to!" But when the corners of his mouth lifted in humorous disbelief of her vehement denial she retorted stiffly, "You cannot think me so naïve, surely? After all the years you've spent living just as you pleased, without a care to the consequences? You must expect then that you've provided a surfeit of gossip that continues to circulate the salons to this day. How then could I not come to hear of them? I cannot keep my hands over my ears the entire time I visit my friends and relations!"

"The salons must be dull indeed if reliving my chequered history is providing the evening's entertainment!"

"If anything, time has merely cemented your reputation. And while most of the protagonists are only too willing to recount those adventures because it gives them the opportunity to boast of the part they played, however insignificant, there is one amongst your previous—um—attachments who—"

"Lovers. Say it as it is."

Estée threw up a plump hand in embarrassed annoyance, several bracelets of milky pearls sliding down her wrist. "Very well. One of your previous *lovers* has taken exception, finding these retellings a painful reminder that she was forsaken most cruelly when you married."

"Forsaken? The rules of such engagements are well known, and affairs conducted accordingly. One cannot cast off what one does not own."

"That may very well be true. I have not the slightest idea what those rules are," she answered primly. "What I do know is that our ancient aunts have warned that you have a disgruntled lover intent on enacting her revenge on you by publicly humiliating your duchess at her presentation. I hope I have not dithered this time."

"That was the exact warning?"

"Yes. *Tante Philippe* repeated it to me *twice*."

The Duke's black eyes glittered. It was one thing for him to deal with those seeking retribution for past transgressions, but something else entirely to involve his wife in their revenge. All pretence of indifference vanished.

"I presume this—er—*warning* is the reason I am here in Paris and not rocking my son's cradle in Versailles?" he asked curtly. When she nodded, he flicked out the skirts of his velvet frock coat and resumed his seat on the chaise. "Tell me everything."

SIX

"L UCIAN SAID you could not put in a letter what you wished to discuss," the Duke continued. "That you suspect your correspondence is being opened by M'sieur Marville?"

"I do not suspect it," Estée replied. "I know it to be so! *Tante Philippe* had the information from a trusted source within Marville's post office."

"And this plot to have revenge on me through Antonia…Was our aunt forthcoming with the name of this disgruntled lover?"

Estée was surprised. "You truly do not know who it is?"

"I own to being omniscient but I cannot read minds."

When his sister remained silent, he looked into her blue eyes and quietly stated the obvious. "I am not about to provide you with a list of my former lovers from which you may choose one. Be specific."

"Oh! I thought you were being circumspect, because it was only a little over a twelvemonth ago that the Comtesse was hanging off your arm at every social gathering. She even had the bad manners to openly gloat, and before me! If you truly have forgotten her, that pleases me beyond words. She is a beautiful feline but has a foul temperament—all hiss and claws and very little purr."

The Duke dared to grin. "That considerably narrows the field. In fact, I know of only one who matches that description." He lost the smile. "But as my life began again when Antonia twirled into it, twelve months ago might as well be ten lifetimes, such is the yawning divide between that life and the life I now lead."

Estée sighed her happiness. "I am glad to hear it! And that is very true. I do wonder from time to time what our days may have been like if not for that fateful night, when you swept into the foyer with Antonia in your arms, she with a bullet in her shoulder, and you as white as a ghost and covered in her blood—"

"Please, Estée, I beg you. That particularly painful memory is not one to which I wish to hold dear. You mentioned a comtesse, and with such a germane description am I to presume we are speaking of Thérèse, Comtesse Duras-Valfons?"

At the name Estée screwed up her little nose as if offended by a unpleasant smell. "We are. *Tante Phillipe* confided that Thérèse's English husband came to her begging she intervene on his behalf to have his wife away from you."

It was news to Roxton.

"Had I known Lord Thesiger had been reduced to begging I would have cut the connection at once."

"Which is why Thérèse went to great lengths to ensure you did not," Estée explained. "And she lied to Thesiger, telling him she had given *you* up, when in fact the reverse was true. When news of your marriage reached Paris, the Marquis de Chesnay dared to read aloud the notice within Thérèse's hearing so that everyone might see her reaction. She did not disappoint. She fainted! That is when her husband, and all Paris, knew she had lied, and that she had fully expected to resume your affair upon your return from England. But I do have some sympathy for her—"

"Your forgiveness is boundless."

"I said *some* sympathy." Adding with a sidelong glance because she dared not look at him directly, "I only hope in my heart of hearts that what she confided in *Tante Philippe* is also a lie. Although it would explain why she fainted and was afterwards distraught. If she told her husband your affair was at an end, but in fact it was not, here would be the proof! And of course he will burn with rage to be publicly humiliated, if she makes good on her threat and offers up this proof to the world, and at Antonia's court presentation no less."

"Estée, I retract what I said about being omniscient. I have no idea what you are blathering on about."

"According to *Tante Philippe,* Thérèse does not care in the least if she embarrasses herself or her husband, and has them both banished. She is determined to have her day in the sun all to ruin Antonia's happiness because she says you ruined hers!"

"Is that supposed to make the situation clearer to me? You have merely smeared more mud on the looking glass."

"Then I am glad I did not put it in a letter and you are here to find out in person. Though it makes the telling that much more distasteful for me."

The Duke frowned. "I do not doubt it." Adding with marked diffidence, because he was discussing a topic he never thought he would ever broach with his sister, "I apologise in advance for dredging up certain particulars of my previous liaisons with you, but needs must… I am at a loss to recall a single circumstance where I gave the Comtesse Duras-Valfons cause to be unhappy. Or, for that matter, that the association had any more substance to it than any such previous connections. I had assumed that we both had entered into it with the usual mutual understanding. I was not her first lover, but," he added, meeting her blue eyes with a small smile, "she was most certainly my last."

"You needn't have said that, *mon cher frère*," Estée murmured, sudden tears behind her eyes and a hand lightly to the velvet cuff of his frock coat. "I know. And so does everyone else."

The Duke nodded and continued, puzzlement still lingering.

"At Fontainebleau, just after Antonia left for England, the Comtesse and I parted on good terms. Or so I had thought. Nothing in her demeanour or her words indicated her displeasure. Why—of what does she accuse me?"

"You truly do not know?"

Roxton threw up a lace-covered wrist in frustration and pulled a face. His expression said it all. He was oblivious. His ignorance should have surprised her. After all, he always had his finger on the pulse of societal gossip, be it here in Paris or in London. She had no way of knowing how he came by his information but suspected he paid for it, as he did everything else in his life, handsomely rewarding those who were loyal to him.

But in this matter concerning the Comtesse Duras-Valfons, she understood his ignorance. To his mind the affair had ended on reasonable terms. Why then would he give it a second thought? Nor would he have considered the possible outcome that most, if not all, men who participated in these games of seduction rarely considered. And that was because Estée believed, and so did Society, it was the female's responsibility to take care of any consequences resulting from illicit affairs.

If a pregnancy resulted then the female quietly retired from Society until after the birth. If the infant lived, it was sent far into the country to an indigent couple, never to be seen again or acknowledged in any way. After a short absence, and with the bloom back in her cheeks, the female re-entered Society. The reason for her absence might be known but if her husband did not acknowledge the infant as his, then Society did not either. It was as if the birth had never occurred. The lovers reunited, or parted and new lovers acquired, the rules obeyed, and the cycle of the pursuit of pleasure continued. No one was shocked. No one complained. No one cared, as long as the matter was dealt with in the usual way —discreetly and without a fuss.

That the Comtesse intended to flout these unwritten rules had so shocked the ancient aunts that their grumbling animosity towards the Duke was temporarily put aside. Roxton's mother, their sister, had been a Salvan. The family name and pride were at stake. What's more he was a good friend of the King. They knew to whom they owed their allegiance.

Astute to the machinations of Society since her first marriage at the age of fifteen, Estée realised there was more at play here than the ancient aunts were letting on. She suspected that they were intriguing with the Comtesse to embarrass her brother, but that they also wished to hedge their bets, and so had no wish to make an enemy of their nephew. Thus they had confided in her, setting her the unpleasant task of informing her brother that one of his previous lovers had recently given birth and was intent on making a public announcement that he was her infant's sire.

"Men are such ignorant creatures about female matters," she said on a shuddering breath, unable to keep the tears from sliding down her cheeks or the sadness from her voice, thinking of Antonia and what this news would mean to her. "For females such matters are all we think about, we must, and often until we are too old to think of anything at all. Perhaps it is because I am *enceinte* that I am more sensitive than Thérèse deserves. I truly do not care for the woman. She knew that should a—ah—*consequence*—arise from your affair it was hers to manage, and discreetly.

"Yet the ancient aunts they tell me Thérèse has chosen to make a-a *fuss*. She intends to use this infant she has birthed to have her revenge on you. For what we ask ourselves? Stupid woman! If she goes through with this-this *plan*, everyone will know her for what she is—an ill-bred, *vengeful* creature unworthy of her lineage. Of course, no one will take her side. But it will cause a sensation, however briefly, because it concerns *you*. Oh, Roxton! When I think of the unnecessary *cruelty* this will inflict on Antonia, who is a new mother herself, it breaks my heart—"

"I do not have another handkerchief to offer you," the Duke interrupted hoarsely, up off the chaise and across the room and at her dressing table. "Which drawer?"

But he was not quick enough. Estée caught a glimpse of his lean handsome face fired red with embarrassment and in the next breath whiter than bleached linen. Such was her shock at his cold horror that she did not answer him until he repeated the question, and more harshly than before.

"ESTÉE! HANDKERCHIEFS! WHICH DRAWER?"

"The bottom one to the far right."

He jerked open the little drawer. It was full of lace-bordered handkerchiefs, but he took his time to extract one. He needed a moment to breathe, to restore his equilibrium, as a mixture of emotions coursed through him and chilled blood.

He was in disbelief, thunderstruck by his ignorance. Wrath welled up within him that the Comtesse would dare to embarrass him in this way; worse—be intent on causing distress to his Duchess. Most of all he had an urgent need for action—to discover the truth for himself. What he intended to do about it was beyond him at that moment. Uppermost in his mind was limiting the damage of the woman's scheming, and before it reached Antonia.

He returned to the chaise and gave Estée the handkerchief, but he did not sit.

"Thank you for telling me. I am sorry our ancient aunts gave you such a distasteful task. Rest assured I will deal with the matter, and swiftly. Now you must excuse me. I am wanted elsewhere."

"You will tell Antonia?"

He looked at her with an expression that told her nothing of his thoughts.

"I will do whatever is necessary to ensure my wife's happiness. As that is what you want too, I know I can rely on your discretion."

"Naturally. I won't say a word."

He inclined his head, and taking a look about the room surprised her by saying conversationally, "You should use the opportunity while you are with us at Versailles to have your apartment redecorated. New wallpaper, carpets, furniture, whatever you wish."

Estée was instantly diverted. She beamed with delight.

"Truly? I was only saying to Lucian a fortnight ago that we should apply to you to do just that, and before the baby arrives in the spring." She regarded him with a mixture of shyness and eagerness. "When you say apartment, you do mean all the rooms—Lucian's, mine, and the baby's too?"

"All of them. The servants' too if required. I shall inform Lapin that he is to give you *carte blanche*. I will leave the two of you to work out the particulars."

Mention of the hôtel's steward had her up off the chaise. Taking his hand, which he had held out in farewell, she startled him by kissing it and then pressing it to her cheek.

"You are the best and most generous of brothers! I could cry with happiness!"

"I do not doubt that, but please restrain yourself," he quipped, gently extracting his fingers. He made her a small bow. "I will be returning to the villa in time for supper, so will say my farewells. Antonia is looking forward to you joining us at the end of the week. I've brought you the large carriage, though you will have to make do with only three of your women, the villa such as it is—"

"Oh that is but a small inconvenience," she replied happily. "The others will have too much to do here, what with the apartment in such an upheaval."

"Yes. I thought that might be the case," he replied, and confident his sister's mind was now firmly directed to the pleasurable feminine pursuit of redecoration, he took his leave.

He had barely turned his back and the liveried footmen opened the double doors, before his sister was calling out loudly for her women. The note of breathless excitement in her tone reassured him that any lingering worry she had about the Comtesse and her scheming had dissolved, transferred to him, any unpleasantness no longer her concern. That had been precisely his aim.

Leaving his sister's apartment, he also left the hôtel and went straight to Rossards. Despite having a whole day of appointments organized by his steward before his return to the villa, he needed a few hours of uncomplicated male company that was to be had at the gaming tables of his favorite bastion of Parisian aristocratic privilege.

It would give him time to reorder his thoughts and decide on a stratagem to deal with Thérèse Duras-Valfons. And if one wanted the latest gossip burning through Parisian salons, it was to be found bright and glowing at Rossards. He would know, just by walking through the establishment's doors, if what the Comtesse had alleged about her infant had gone beyond the shocked whisperings of his ancient aunts.

Regardless of the outcome of that reception, how he would broach the subject with Antonia he had not a clue.

SEVEN

VILLA ROXTON, RUE DES RÉSERVOIRS, PETIT PARC, VERSAILLES.

Antonia stepped away from the fireplace and spun about with a triumphant smile. She addressed the three gentlemen who were looking up at two half-length portraits newly hooked side-by-side above the painted mantel. One was of a handsome nobleman, the other of his beautiful young wife. They wore the hairstyles and clothing fashionable during the Regency of the Duc d'Orleans, and had been painted by Hyacinthe Rigaud, the most celebrated artist of his generation.

"Is this not the perfect place for them to be reunited?"

"It is, Mme la Duchesse," Martin Ellicott agreed, taking a step closer, gaze on the paintings. "I do not believe I have seen these particular pictures of M'sieur le Marquis and Mme la Marquise before today. They are a splendid pair."

"Is that who they are?" Lord Vallentine remarked with a lift of his cleft chin. "Thought they looked vaguely familiar. The nose on him, and her blue eyes had me wonderin'."

"Lucian! You are deliberately being foolish to annoy me," Antonia said without heat, returning to look up at the portraits. "You know very well who they are! M'sieur le Duc has his father's fine nose. And Madame, she has her mother's beautiful blue eyes. And you have seen Monseigneur's parents before, in the big family picture hanging in the Long Gallery at Treat. But these portraits they were painted just after they were married. That is what Jean-Luc he told me."

She went over to the Duke, who had yet to comment. He had not taken his gaze from the portraits since entering the room. The last to arrive for supper, returning from Paris on horseback, he had taken a bath and was dressed *en déshabillé*, in a Chinese silk banyan over a fresh white shirt and velvet breeches.

Antonia guessed by his faraway look that he was remembering a time when his parents were still alive. She caught at his fingers and that broke the spell.

"Are you pleased to see them restored to their rightful place?"

Roxton smiled down at her.

"I am. Though I cannot say I remember these particular portraits, or what wall they graced. Though I suspect it was not in this room."

"Because this was your parents' bedchamber before you had the house remodelled, yes?" When he nodded, she said, "Jean-Luc he cannot recall precisely which wall either, but I told him that was unimportant. I would not have known these portraits existed before today had he and I not spoken in the garden. And he agreed with me that as this was their bedchamber, and we now use it for breakfast and supper, it is fitting to have your parents here with us. But mostly for Julian, so he will know his grandparents when he is older."

Her gaze flickered about the white-washed panelled room with its high plastered ceiling, and fixed on the French doors that opened out onto a small private garden, the blue velvet curtains tied back to allow a view of the fast-fading light of a winter's day.

"Your parents must have had a very nice apartment here," she said wistfully.

"But so do we, do we not, with a lovely prospect over *Sa Majesté's* parkland from our windows on the first floor."

"We do. And at this time of year, with the morning mist in the trees it is very beautiful. But in the spring, this room, with the doors opened wide, would fill with the scent from the flowerbeds. I am very sure your mother she would have found that enchanting."

The Duke drew up her hand to kiss. "If we are in residence when there are blooms, I shall have them put in vases and brought up to your dressing room."

Antonia went on tiptoe and kissed his cheek. "Thank you, Monseigneur, but let us keep the blooms in the garden and we can take a walk amongst their perfume after our breakfast." She had a sudden thought, a crease between her brows. "It is usual here in France for the masters of great houses to have their bedchambers on the ground floor, and yet here at the villa, and at the hôtel, too, we do not. Is that not strange?"

"Strange, *ma belle*? Not when I am partial to the English preference for bedchambers being off the ground floor and—"

"Wise," Lord Vallentine interrupted darkly. "Havin' only a set of flimsy French doors between bed and garden is askin' for trouble. Far more secure to be up a flight of stairs. That discourages trespass, and with men on every landin', we all get to sleep soundly."

"No one who is not meant to be here would dare set foot on M'sieur le Duc's property," Antonia said dismissively, taking her place at the round table, set with the necessary silver and porcelain for supper. A liveried footman pulled out her chair. "And even if we were to sleep down here, there are enough men in our garden to frighten away any daring trespasser." She chuckled. "I am very sure those in the house next to ours must wonder if Monseigneur he does have his own army with the number of servants that we keep!"

Lord Vallentine, who was already at the sideboard and had

filled a bowl with soup and was now piling a plate with a selection of meats, fruits, and pastries, looked over his shoulder, and said with a huff, "It *is* an army! And why not? They have their orders, and woe betide if even the tenants over the wall were fool enough to lift the gate latch without permission. This lot would be onto 'em *subito*."

Antonia frowned. "I do not understand. You talk as if we are not safe in our own home. And why would our neighbors visit via the garden gate? I am told the house it was recently leased to a family with three daughters who—" She looked to the Duke with alarm. "Renard? Has there been a trespasser in our garden?"

"In the garden? Not that I am aware, *ma vie*," Roxton replied smoothly, a nod to his butler to pour out the coffee. "I do not believe Lucian meant that there is any immediate danger in the literal sense. Nor—I am certain he will be only too willing to assure you—did he wish to cause you any unnecessary disquiet, or worry for the welfare of our son—"

"Eh? A'course not!" Vallentine blustered when the Duke stared at him with a lift of his brows. "It's just that like Roxton here, I've got an Englishman's aversion for sleepin' quarters bein' located close to the earth." He plonked his heavily laden plate and a bowl of cream of oyster soup on the table and straddled a chair. "These Frenchies they can stick their bedchambers where they please, and good luck to 'em I say, but for this Englishman my bed's up a flight of stairs and down a passageway, with plenty of men in-between. That's all there is to it."

"This aversion for the earth must be troubling indeed for you, Lucian," Antonia said smoothly, glancing suspiciously from her brother-in-law to her husband, and thinking there was more to the topic of a trespasser than either was willing to divulge. "For how is it that the greatest swordsman in all France and England needs to sleep upstairs, and with men guarding the stairs, to feel safe?"

Rather than dispelling her suspicion, His Lordship confirmed it when he mumbled a non-committal response before putting his head down to concentrate on slurping his soup. Antonia would have persisted had not Martin Ellicott taken the opportunity in the ensuing slurpy silence to divert her by changing the topic.

Martin waited until a footman had filled her dish with coffee, and then asked lightly, silver soup spoon suspended over a bowl of chicken and vegetable broth,"Mme la Duchesse, you mentioned that the portraits of M'sieur et Mme le Marquis were discovered…?" and was forced to suppress a smile when the Duke threw him a look of gratitude.

"Oh yes! I was about to tell you all about the discovery and my meeting with Jean-Luc in the garden, but then Lucian he had me worrying about a trespasser—"

"I had you wor—? Oh, all right," His Lordship muttered when the Duke's gaze shot to the ceiling. "My apologies." He raised his silver soup spoon to the Duchess. "I'm all ears. Particularly as I'm sure we'd all like to know how this Luc fellow got into the garden in the first place."

"You think Jean-Luc he is a trespasser?" she teased, and shook her head, a glance at the Duke. "You may rest easy, *mon beau-frère*. Jean-Luc he did not enter our garden by unlatching the gate. He has been of service to Monseigneur's family since—"

"Ha! I should've guessed he was a servant," Vallentine burst out with relief. "But the word *meetin'* threw me." Saying as an aside to the Duke, "You must have the only duchess in all of Europe who attempts to carry on a genuine conversation with a lackey—"

"*Attempt?*" Antonia retorted, finally provoked. "You think those in our employ do not have a brain?"

"Well? Do they?" Vallentine goaded, and with a sly grin went back to slurping his soup.

Antonia sat up, but this time she did not take the bait. Instead she said with deceptive sweetness, "Lucian, I hope you are not suggesting Monseigneur would allow his family to be cared for by imbeciles or the mentally deranged?"

"Eh!? Mentally de—de-*ranged*? I never—now steady on! Don't you go puttin' words in m'mouth, or thoughts into Roxton's head," Vallentine demanded. "That's not what I meant at all, and you know it!" He then ruined his bluff of confidence by leaning in to the Duke and saying meekly, "It's not what I meant."

"What I know, my dear," the Duke replied evenly, attention on finely slicing up a pear, "is that by questioning the Duchess, it appears that is exactly what you do mean."

Vallentine muttered something about being a fish and swallowing the hook dangling before his eyes. He pushed aside his empty soup bowl to put in its place the heavily laden plate of assorted cheeses, meats, and pastries.

"I deliberately did not use the word lackey, Vallentine," Antonia countered. "Because Jean-Luc he is not one. Is he, Monseigneur?"

The Duke speared a thin slice of pear with his fork and slowly lifted his gaze to Antonia's green eyes. His expression gave nothing away of his thoughts. "Please do not keep Martin waiting, *mignonne*, and answer his question about where the portraits were discovered."

She instantly knew he was evading her question, but before she could reply Vallentine broke into their moment. He was oblivious to the Duke's pointed attempt to turn the conversation.

"But if this Luc fellow ain't a lackey, and you say he's not a trespasser, then who the devil is he, and what was he doin' in the garden?"

There was a moment's silence. The Duke and Duchess had locked eyes. Speech was unnecessary to communicate their thoughts to one another, Antonia made aware that the subject of Jean-Luc was not one her husband wished to discuss there and then. This surprised her, but she acquiesced to his silent request.

"Jean-Luc was in the garden with the other servants for the household servant audit—"

"Ah! So he *is* a servant!" Vallentine announced.

Again Antonia looked to the Duke to comment but he had dropped his gaze and returned to consuming the slices of pear. It was left to Martin Ellicott to gauge the mood and move the conversation forward, and in another direction.

"Is this the audit being conducted by Mercier, M'sieur le Duc?" Martin Ellicott asked.

"It is," Roxton replied, but he still did not look up, as if the slices of pear required all his attention.

The Duchess and Martin Ellicott, who were both looking at the Duke, happened to glance at one another, and they knew from their respective expressions what the other was thinking: Something was amiss with the Duke. His Lordship, however, was oblivious. His ignorance helped lighten the mood.

"Mercier?" Vallentine pounced on the name of the villa's major-domo. When Antonia nodded he leaned in again to the Duke and said in an under-voice, "Good man is Mercier—he'll ferret out any spongers and misplaced inquisitors—"

"He will, Lucian," agreed the Duke, cutting him off. He glanced up from his plate to smile at his wife. "*Mignonne*, Martin is not the only one who wishes to know where the portraits were discovered. And Lucian will not interrupt again—"

"Blast! There I go again!"

"And again," quipped the Duke.

"I am sorry, Monseigneur, but how am I to tell you about the discovery of the portraits without mentioning how it is I came to speak at length with Jean-Luc in the garden?" Antonia replied, and smiled softly. "The one cannot be untangled from the other, yes?"

"I'm sure you will find way," the Duke stated flatly, setting aside his pear knife and plate and taking up his dish of coffee, gaze remaining anywhere but on his wife.

Antonia was silent and thoughtful. She was now convinced something was greatly troubling the Duke. And whatever it was, it had happened while he was in Paris, for he had returned to the villa in a different mood from the one he had been in when he had departed at first light. She pondered what it could be, wondering if there was some news about his sister he did not wish to share. But she instantly dismissed this. If Estée or her baby were in any distress the Duke would not be here but still in Paris, and Vallentine called to his wife's side. So, no; his distraction had nothing to do with his sister's well-being. But what then could it be…?

EIGHT

Martin Ellicott addressed the Duchess, jolting Antonia from her thoughts and bringing her back to the table.

"Today was a particularly lovely day to be out of doors, Mme la Duchesse," he commented conversationally, smiling across at her without a glance at the Duke. "So I do not doubt the servants enjoyed their time in the sun as much as you and his little lordship…?"

"That is why I took Julian out into the garden," Antonia replied. And taking her cue from him she continued in a light conversational tone, hoping it might bring the Duke out of his abstraction. "My women they were against the idea of Julian being out in the winter air, saying it was bad for an infant. But his wet nurses assured me they sit in the winter sun with their own infants, and so why should not Julian also? And so I insisted. But what did my women make the nursemaids do with my son?" she added, eyes widening as she looked about at the diners. "They had them wrap him in so many layers that he looked like a big juicy sugar-plum!" When there was general chuckling she smiled. "It is true I tell you! I had them remove half of his wrappings, but to stop their agitation I put Julian inside my muff—"

"*Wh-What?* You put him—You put your son *into* your *muff?*" Vallentine repeated, agog. When Antonia nodded he gave a snort of laughter, and slapped his hand on the table, and so hard the crystal glasses tinkled. "Well a'course you would! I wager he was as warm as toast in there." He frowned suddenly, and had to ask, "But how did he breathe?"

"Silly! He did not go in head first. His head it poked out at one end, and his little feet they barely stuck out the other, so it was his little belly that was warmest."

Vallentine screwed up his nose in thought. "I trust he was wearin' his pilch and clout. Y' wouldn't want any nasty surprises left in your muff. On the other hand, if he were left free and easy in the breeze it would make for less clean up."

"Why is it your head it is constantly full of trivialities?" Antonia demanded without heat.

"Trivial? You might think it so when your son has a battalion of nursemaids to clean up after him day and night. But the rest of us—particularly those of us who have their own bundle of joy on the way—we worry about all sorts of mundane details you might think nonsensical."

Antonia looked at him over the gold rim of her porcelain coffee dish with a lift of her brows and baited him.

"Do you see M'sieur le Duc concerning himself with these nonsensical details? No! Because they are unimportant. And as he has told you before, he leaves such details to those who are most expert. Is that not so, Monseigneur?"

"Just so, *ma vie*," said the Duke, making motions to rise. But when Antonia continued, he settled again and politely waited for her to finish her explanation.

"But because I know you will ask it of me anyway, Vallentine," she said with a sigh, "let me put your mind at rest. Julian he was not only in his pilch and clout, but wearing a bonnet, and woollen stockings. My muff was for extra warmth without the bulk." She smiled with pride, her dimple showing. "Which was very clever of me, and an ingenious alternative to Julian looking like a sugar-plum *bébé*, was it not?"

"Inspired, *ma belle*," agreed the Duke, and once again went to stand. Yet when Martin Ellicott asked the Duchess a question, again he settled to await her response.

"Mme la Duchesse, was it when you were strolling the garden with His little Lordship in your muff that you happened upon Jean-Luc?"

"Yes!"

Her smile and look at Martin told him she was grateful for his question. He also got the distinct impression there was something underlying in her conversation she wished the Duke to understand.

"Julian he lost one of his stockings and Jean-Luc he retrieved it. He had been waiting in line with the servants to be interviewed by M'sieur Mercier. But seeing the moment Julian kicked off his stocking he picked it up and went to return it. But my women they stopped him, saying it was not his place to approach me and hand me things. Imagine how ridiculous this notion was to me when everyone knows Jean-Luc he is the one who goes back and forth to the hôtel to fetch my books.

"And when my women kept making a fuss, two of the footmen came over, thinking poor Jean-Luc he was causing a disturbance. Which he was not. And then M'sieur Mercier he joined us. That's when I became angry." She confessed to the Duke, annoyed with herself, "I raised my voice, Renard—which I do not like doing in the least—and told them all to go away and leave us alone. I upset Julian. He has never heard his Maman be angry." She put out her hand, and the Duke covered it with his own. "You never raise your voice with anyone, even when I know you are furious, and everyone they do as they are told."

"It is a practised—er—art. And I have had many more years'

experience than you." The Duke gently squeezed her fingers. "I do not doubt that in spite of your annoyance at wishing to be heard you handled the situation with aplomb."

"I hope that is so," Antonia said with a smile, not entirely convinced. "I had Gabrielle take Julian and my women to the far end of the garden, because no one could hear over his crying. And he would not stop, even when I covered his face with my kisses. So I must truly have startled him. I startled everyone! M'sieur Mercier fled back to his desk with the footmen, and Jean-Luc shuffled away. But I called him back." She looked about the table and included the others in their conversation. "I wanted to thank him for not only retrieving Julian's stocking, but also because of all the endless errands I send him on and never once has he complained."

"Does he have reason to complain?" Roxton asked, surprised. "I do not doubt that your errands give him occupation—"

"That is what he said!" Antonia exclaimed happily. "That my book lists give him a reason to visit the hôtel, and spend a few hours there, in the library, perusing the shelves."

"He does not need a reason. He can visit the library, and the hôtel, whenever he chooses."

Antonia held the Duke's gaze. "Jean-Luc said that too. Not about having a reason, but that while he might live here at the villa, he has permission to come and go to the hôtel as he pleases. This intrigued me. And because he is old, I wondered if perhaps he had been a servant and was now retired from his duties and lived here at your largesse. So naturally I asked him. Why would I not? As your duchess I need to know these things, yes? And Jean-Luc he obliged me."

Despite his moody preoccupation, the Duke could not help smiling.

"I do not doubt that you managed to extract his *entire* life story," he replied as he finally rose from his chair. "Which leaves me nothing to add… and as the clocks are about to chime the hour and I still have letters to write, you will have to excuse me. I am pleased you were able to enjoy the garden in the winter sunshine, *ma vie*," he added gently. "I only wish I had been here to enjoy it with you."

"I wish that too…" Antonia replied with a smile, then forced herself to say lightly, "Monseigneur, I have yet to answer Martin's question. Do you not want to hear what Jean-Luc he told me about the lovely portraits of your parents?"

"Not tonight. I will await that pleasure if and when you care to repeat it—perhaps at breakfast."

The Duke had barely turned a shoulder when Antonia said very quietly, causing him to turn back to meet her gaze,

"Pardon, M'sieur le Duc, I do not wish to keep you from your letters but first will you please assure me that you do not feel as others do about your duchess sitting in the sunshine with Jean-Luc Levron—"

"*Levron*?" Lord Vallentine blurted out, giving a start. "Is that the Jean-Luc you've been chatterin' with in the winter sunshine?" When Antonia nodded, he looked to the Duke and then back at her, and rolled his eyes on a huff. "No wonder the servants were jittery. Duchesses don't ask the Jean-Lucs of this world their life story. And they certainly don't sit with 'em in the sun. It just ain't done."

Antonia sat up tall. "Well this duchess did and she intends to do it again!"

NINE

"Begone," ordered the Duke, following up his command with a jerk of his head toward the door. His butler and the footmen filed out, leaving the diners alone. He did not return to his seat but stood at his chair and cast an eye over his family, who were all looking at him expectantly.

"Martin! What do you know of Jean-Luc Levron's history?"

Martin Ellicott was surprised to be first addressed but he answered the Duke calmly.

"M'sieur Levron holds the position of assistant to M'sieur Darville, the *bibliothécaire* within your household, M'sieur le Duc. A position he has had for a number of years. That is all I kn—"

"No. That is *not* all you know," the Duke enunciated through his teeth. "That is the porridge served up to guests and any intermeddler who has the impertinence to ask."

This uncharacteristically harsh response to a rather innocuous reply was puzzling and put everyone on the alert. Furtive glances went round the table and no one spoke. The Duke hardly noticed, or drew breath.

"But within any of my households, I would wager there isn't a man or woman who doesn't know from which side of the blanket M'sieur Levron emerged. Even if they know nothing else about him, or his long personal history after he came into the world, they know that much. They know him for a—*bastard*."

He looked across at Antonia then, and to her it was as if he was looking through her for there was none of the usual softening of his features or his voice when he addressed her.

"And today Mme la Duchesse discovered for herself that Jean-Luc Levron, the old man who comes and goes with her books, is *of* my family but he is not *part* of it. And he will never be part of it. He cannot. But he is under my protection, not because I wish it but because my father in his will consigned Jean-Luc Levron into my care. I *inherited* him as one does an old chair favored by a parent, and so no one dares to throw it out!

"I will honor my father's wishes and care for Levron until his last breath. He is a good and decent man. That is not in dispute. But I am not my father, and my father was never duke. I am, and just as the fourth duke did before me, and for the welfare of my son and heirs, the existence of base blood connections will never be acknowledged. *Ever*. And *that* you may take as my last word on the matter, and on the existence of Jean-Luc Levron. I bid you all a goodnight."

He politely inclined his head, turned on a heel, and swept from the room to a pin-dropping silence.

"Damme! I've rarely, if ever, seen him in such a fury!" Vallentine announced in amazement, a few moments after the door closed on the Duke's back. He jumped up and fetched the silver coffeepot from the sideboard. He held it up. Antonia and Martin both nodded and pushed out their dishes to be refilled. Pouring into Antonia's dish he said gently, "Best give him until mornin' to cool his coals, eh?" When she blinked up at him he winked and added bashfully, "That's what I do with his sister when she's had a fit of the sullens. She always comes right by mornin'. He will too. You'll see."

"Thank you for the advice, Lucian," Antonia replied quietly, still distracted. "But Monseigneur he does not have fits of any kind." She sipped at her coffee in thought. "There is something— something is bothering him—something I do not understand… Do you see it too, Martin?"

"I do, Mme la Duchesse," Martin Ellicott said without hesitation. "For M'sieur le Duc to show such suppressed emotion is rare. I have only seen it upon one other occasion—"

"When?" demanded His Lordship.

"The night he was forced to send Mme la Duchesse to her grandmother in England."

"That was a very bad time for both of us," Antonia murmured, and gave a little shudder as if shaking off the memory.

"Perhaps what he needs is a good leechin' to release whatever ill-humors *are* botherin' him?" Vallentine offered teasingly with a wink.

Antonia giggled at the image of the Duke pulling a face of disgust at Vallentine's suggestion. She shook her head with a smile.

"*Merci, mon cher beau-frère*, for making me laugh. But no." She lost her smile. "You know, as Martin does, as do I, that M'sieur le Duc he is not ill. He is worried. I see it in his eyes. So very worried —but about what?"

"Worried?" His Lordship gave a huff. "Is that what you call his reaction to findin' out you'd been chatterin' away to Levron? Personally, I don't know what there is to concern himself in that. For a pig-widgeon, the old man's harmless enough—"

"What is this pig—*pig*-widgeon?"

"Pig-widgeon? Oh! Ah! Um. Er. A-a—noodle. Anyway, that's the common whisper. But I don't rightly know because I've never actually said more than two words to him. And come to think on it, I can't remember what those two words are now. Whenever I've wandered into the library and he's there, he puts his head down and shuffles away."

"Telling me Jean-Luc he is a pig-widgeon and a noodle is of no help to me at all, Lucian. Martin, do you know what—"

"Not fully *compos mentis*," Lord Vallentine enunciated, and to stress his point he made a circular motion with his index finger in the air near his ear and pulled a face.

"Oh! They are disparaging terms for someone who is a simpleton, yes?" Antonia stated. When His Lordship nodded she added seriously, "But Jean-Luc he is not simple in the way a fool who is born simple. He merely requires the time, and our patience, so he can form his words. I have seen this condition before, when I lived with *mon père*. There was a boy—Ricardo— who lived across the street from our villa. His stutter it was very bad, and if people they did not give him time to form his words, he could not speak at all! But *mon père* showed him kindness and was very patient with him, and so Ricardo's stutter it was not so bad.

"It is the same with Jean-Luc. But he did not have this stutter from birth as Ricardo did. Jean-Luc he tells me that when he was a youth attending the Sorbonne he was struck down by a carriage while crossing the *Pont Royal*. His head hit the cobbles, and he broke his arm. When he woke, he was not the same. It took him many months to recover. And while his bones mended, he was left with a crooked arm. And he had acquired a stutter. *Et voilà!*"

"So I was right about him being a bit soft in the head," Lord Vallentine stated.

"No, because Jean-Luc he is not simple," Antonia mildly scolded. "His brain does not work as well as it did." She let out a breath. "Sadly, the hit to the head put an end to his studies, and his wish to be an *avocat*." She smiled at Martin. "As Monseigneur will not talk about Jean-Luc Levron perhaps you can tell me what you know about his family."

Martin was surprised. "Of course, Mme la Duchesse. But he—

Jean-Luc did he not, as M'sieur le Duc surmised, tell you his life story while you were out in the garden?"

Antonia shook her head. "How could he do that when M'sieur Mercier and the footmen, and my silly ladies, all scared him sufficiently that he could not speak at all for several minutes! Which is why I had him sit on the bench beside me. To make him comfortable again, I told him about the history I am presently reading. And when he was himself and at his ease he asked if I would like to see the portraits of Monseigneur's parents. He had taken it upon himself to care for all the pictures in this house, but those particular pictures he kept in his rooms above the stables. I must have looked concerned because he assured me that his apartment is well appointed and has its own heater, so any pictures and books he keeps there are well preserved. Of course my concern was for him, but no matter. He was the one who suggested Monseigneur's parents hang here in the breakfast room."

Vallentine glanced at the portraits above the mantel then looked from the Duchess to Martin Ellicott and back again, baffled.

"So Levron didn't mention his parents?"

"The first I heard of Jean-Luc being from the wrong side of the pillow—"

"Blanket, Mme la Duchesse," Martin corrected gently, adding with a diffident smile, "Though I think it hardly matters which article of bedding is used for the euphemism, such as it is."

"Blanket? Oh! *Merci. Oui*, the wrong side of the blanket," Antonia repeated, as if committing it to memory. "Lucian, I was not aware of Jean-Luc's unfortunate parentage until Monseigneur mentioned the blanket, and used that terrible word—"

"Bastard? Well, yes, it isn't a pleasant word," Vallentine agreed. "But that's what he is. An infant born the wrong side of the blanket, or if you want to be proper about it—*out of wedlock*—is commonly referred to as a bastard."

"I do know the meaning of the word, Lucian. And it may be

correct, but please do not say it again to me because when it is said so bluntly, or in the way Monseigneur said it, it is a hateful word I do not like in the least!"

When Lord Vallentine inclined his head in assent, she added earnestly, "These babies they did not ask to be born, *n'est-ce pas?* And they most certainly did not ask for parents who were unmarried. *Mon père* spent many years bringing such infants into the world, and it saddened him that the sins of the parents were visited on innocents who would suffer all their lives because of the stigma of their birth."

"Mme la Duchesse, your father was an enlightened and compassionate physician," Martin said gently. "I wish I had known him."

"He was, and I wish that you had been known to each other. I miss him every day... *Mon père* said to me that the mothers of these infants paid the price for their sins by having to give up their babies to orphanages, never to be seen again. Can you imagine? To give up the infant you have carried inside you for nine months? At the time I was too young to truly understand. But now..." Her green eyes filled with tears which she quickly wiped away. "Now I have Julian I could not imagine a worse fate than giving him up and never seeing him again—"

"You need never imagine it, Mme la Duchesse," Martin reassured her. "You will always have his little lordship."

"Yes. Forgive me for being *larmoyante.*" She gave herself a mental shake and said, "*Mon père* was most critical of the absent papas who inflicted this sad choice upon these women, and the life-long stigma on these unwanted infants. Where were these men after they had taken their pleasures? Gone into the night—" She clapped her hands. "Poof! Never to be seen again. They—"

"Hang on a moment, *ma belle-sœur,*" Lord Vallentine interrupted, bright red about the ears. "*Inflict* is rather a rich word and it's makin' this stew of yours a bit thick! Your papa couldn't know for a certainty that *all* these men were care-for-nobody lechers!

And before you argue the point with me, I wish to announce that this topic is an unsavory one for us to be discussin' with *you*, even if your papa was a great physician who delivered hundreds of these infants. Estée would box m' ears if she knew, and Roxton'd be worse than furious, he'd be—

"*Mon père* and I we talked about everything," Antonia said loftily. "No topic was off the list. It is the same with Monseigneur. I may ask him anything."

"*Him*, yes. He's your husband. Just as the physician was your father. Both have say over what you can and cannot know. But it's not the same with *us*."

Antonia shrugged a shoulder, unperturbed. "That may be so, but my father is no more, and my husband he is not here. And as I need to know these things," she added with a sweet smile, "who better to ask if not the two men closest to me after my husband? M'sieur le Duc has forbidden us to talk about Jean-Luc with him, so we must talk amongst ourselves. It is too bad. I would prefer to talk to Monseigneur, but he has said no."

"He might change his mind tomorrow," Vallentine suggested lamely.

"No. I know him. He will not."

Vallentine could see Antonia was going to be stubborn. A sidelong glance at Martin Ellicott, who was as unflustered as always, and he shrugged, blew out his lips and said on a sigh, "Very well. If you need answers, best they come from me or Ellicott than anyone else…And before you go on, I agree with you. Infants are born innocent. But the problem for most about infants born out of wedlock and who are abandoned, are that they become wards of the parish. Least that's what happens in England. I daresay here they are put into orphanages run by one of the Papist orders. Still. It's the same outcome. Someone has to pay for their upkeep. And that falls back on the good people of a parish. It's understandable that those who do right and marry and look after their offspring resent takin' on the care and feedin' of by-blows—

"Bye blows? What is a—"

"Another word for the word you do not like, Mme la Duchesse," Martin interrupted.

"Thing is," Lord Vallentine continued, "while I have nothin' against these women who find themselves pregnant and unmarried, or their babies, I object to you loadin' all the probable papas into the same boat. Think on it a moment. How many of these potential papas give a thought to what could result nine months hence from one of their—um—intimate encounters? There isn't a man on this earth who's thinkin' about *that* when they are—when they are—Damme! You know what I'm gettin' at!"

Antonia opened wide her green eyes. "When they are…?"

Yet when His Lordship stumbled over his words and his pallor turned a deep shade of red, she lost her expression of innocent enquiry and forced down a giggle to look her most contrite. She touched his velvet cuff.

"I am sorry. I did not mean to make you uncomfortable. I am not naïve. When two people are in the throes of a grand passion the consequences are not thought of at all. But what is incomprehensible to me is that in these more enlightened times it is somehow the fault of the infants for being born at all! How is that so? That is not logical." She cocked her head in thought. "Monseigneur and I have spoken about this very thing before, so why, upon this occasion, should he not wish to talk about Jean-Luc?"

Martin Ellicott coughed politely into his fist. "Mme la Duchesse, perhaps that is because it is one thing to discuss matters in a general sense, but quite another when that matter becomes personal in nature."

"But I do not care in the least that Jean-Luc Levron he is illegitimate."

"You may not, Mme la Duchesse, but M'sieur le Duc does, and it would seem, deeply," Martin stated.

Antonia was surprised. "How is it that such a great rake as Monseigneur should of a sudden become prim!?"

Martin grinned and shook his head. "Shall I fetch you a looking-glass, Mme la Duchesse?"

"A looking gla—" Antonia's eyes widened. "*Ça alors!* How silly of me! *Bien sûr! C'est parfaitement logique.* Oh, I must be tired not to have thought of that! Thank you, Martin." She glanced at Lord Vallentine. "And because I am tired, I do not want to make any more guesses. So! One of you please tell me about Jean-Luc's parents."

"His papa wasn't in your boat of probable papas, that's certain," Vallentine volunteered. "From the little I know, Roxton's papa acknowledged Levron from the outset—"

Antonia gasped. "Jean-Luc's papa is also Monseigneur's papa? *Incroyable!* How did I not think this? If that is so, then they are half-brother—"

"Not in Roxton's book they ain't," Vallentine interrupted darkly. "And if you take my advice, you won't mention the connection in those terms to your duke. Before she became the mistress of the Marquis of Alston, Levron's mother was a *marionnettiste* with a traveling fair from the French provinces. Roxton's maman was the daughter of the Comte de Salvan, and the Salvan blood is about as soaked in French *noblesse* as one gets, and she was His Lordship's wife. Two females in possession of such different lineages that one might as well have come from the moon, and t'other from the sun!"

Antonia frowned. As if reading her mind, Martin Ellicott stepped into the silence to offer further explanation to Lord Vallentine's revelation.

"Lord Alston's *connection* with both females—wife and mistress—regardless of their origins—high and low—did not take place concurrently, Mme la Duchesse. I do not know the year of Jean-Luc Levron's birth, but it is quite possible that he is some twenty years older than M'sieur le Duc. As you know Lord Alston did not marry until his thirty-eighth year." He smiled softly at the Duchesse. "And when he did marry it was for love. He was a devoted husband to his young wife."

Antonia unconsciously breathed easy, and finally she smiled brightly.

"*Merci*, Martin. Monseigneur he did tell me about his parents, and their elopement, but Vallentine's mention of the *marionnettiste* confused me—but only for a moment—but no more! All of this is most interesting, and I am pleased to know more about Jean-Luc and his connection to our household, even if his existence it makes Monseigneur uncomfortable. *Ce qui doit être, sera.*" She shook her head. "Yet despite not wishing to talk about Jean-Luc coming from the wrong side of the blanket, I do not think he is the reason for M'sieur le Duc's present worry."

She looked at Martin Ellicott for confirmation.

"I believe you to be right, again, Mme la Duchesse."

Lord Vallentine was baffled. "How can you agree with the Duchess, when we all heard Roxton's speech about Levron, *and* his warning never to talk about him again. It's as clear as peerin' through a quizzing glass to me that Roxton ain't worried, he's spittin' hellfire over it!"

Antonia patted Vallentine's velvet sleeve affectionately.

"Lucian, I do not doubt that you are a great player of draughts, but you are not so good at chess, yes?"

"What's draughts got to do with it?" And when Antonia stifled a smile, his eyes narrowed to slits. "What's Roxton been tellin' you, eh? He always wins at both. But if you must know, I do prefer draughts. I can't sit still long enough to play a decent game of chess."

"Thank you for making me less worried. But you will have to believe me when I say that I know what I am talking about when it concerns M'sieur le Duc."

Just then the clock on the mantel chimed the hour. Mechanically, and stifling a yawn, Antonia stood. Vallentine and Martin did likewise, and they followed her out of the room and down the enfilade to the main staircase.

"I will see you both in the Gallery tomorrow after breakfast," she told them, stopping in a pool of light cast by a wall sconce at the base of the curved stairs. "M'sieur Beauchamp is returning—"

"What? Not another blasted rehearsal?" Vallentine whined.

"It is most necessary. Do you want to see me trip over my feet before Their Majesties and embarrass not only myself but M'sieur le Duc? No. So I practice, and practice some more, and you must help me."

"But I get to be Louis tomorrow, and he gets to be queen!" Vallentine demanded, stabbing a finger in Martin Ellicott's direction. "I'm done with flutterin' a fan!"

Martin and Antonia exchanged a look, and had to look away for fear of bursting into laughter.

"That is a great shame, Lucian, because you flutter a fan very well indeed," Antonia told him in a steady voice. "Your wrist work it is better than the real queen's, and I do not doubt most of the women of the court. I am certain of it."

"An expert flutterer to be sure!" Martin Ellicott chimed in.

His Lordship was momentarily proud and put up his chin, but he was not entirely credulous. "You can flatter me all you want, but it won't change a thing. Tomorrow I'll be the one leanin' m' royal elbow on the mantel bein' Louis while you practice curtseying before my august personage. And Ellicott here will flutter a fan very prettily as my queen. No arguments!"

Martin held out the skirts of his frock coat and executed a neat curtsey. "You will receive none from me, *Votre Majesté*. It will be my very great honor and pleasure to be your queen."

And with that he bowed, said good night, and went on up the stairs with a spring in his step, leaving His Lordship to stare after him, mouth at half-cock, and Antonia with a hand clapped over her mouth and her shoulders shaking with the giggles.

TEN

ANTONIA WOKE in the small hours to find herself alone in the big bed. It was not uncommon for the Duke to wake in the night and pad through to his closet to his escritoire, to read unopened correspondence and to write letters. Sometimes he went down to the library. And when he returned, he would snuggle in and sleep for a few more hours. What was different this time alarmed her. His side of the mattress and his pillows were untouched. He had not been to bed at all.

Throwing a diaphanous silk banyan over her sheer cotton nightshift, she slipped stockinged feet into a pair of fabric mules beside the bed, and went through to her closet. Here she splashed water on her face and rebraided her waist-length hair, tying it off with a satin ribbon she found amongst the clutter on her dressing table.

One of her ladies, whose turn it was to sleep in the small chamber off her mistress's closet, poked her head around the tapestry *portière*. Antonia told her to go back to bed then left the apartment in search of her duke, a chamber stick lighting her way.

She took the secret stair to the library, but he was not there, so back up the stair she went and down the enfilade to his closet, barely noticing the sleeping footmen on chairs in alcoves who were instantly awake and scrambling to their feet as she passed.

There was evidence he had been at his escritoire. A small bundle of sealed letters was on a salver, ready for the morning courier. And by the gold candelabrum with its snuffed candles, was a tray with the remains of a late meal. This did not surprise her because he had eaten only a sliced pear at supper. The coffee pot was cold, so it was some time since he'd been there. The gold and enamel clock on his desk told her there was an hour before dawn.

So where could he be? She knew where she would be, and so there she went, and it was there where she found him.

THE NURSERY GALLERY was snugly warm, its sleeping occupants bathed in the soft orange glow of minimal candlelight necessary to provide comfort and still allow the servants to see and move about with least disturbance. It was eerily quiet. The night nurses were dozing under coverlets in wicker chairs close to their young charges, while nurserymaids and the older children were asleep on cots behind screens. Footmen at either end of the long room were up out of their chairs, to attention at the double doors, no doubt due to the unaccustomed presence of their ducal master.

The Duke was standing by his son's ornate cradle, the silk embroidered curtain of the canopy pulled back and away so he could best view the tiny sleeping occupant tucked up amongst the soft white bedding. And so thoroughly absorbed was he in gazing upon his son that he was unaware he was no longer alone.

Antonia went straight up to him and tucked her hand in his. At her touch, he slowly turned and looked down. She knew he had been far away with his thoughts because recognition was not immediate. He blinked. Then he smiled and drew up her fingers to kiss, before returning to gaze at their infant. He did not speak for several moments. And when he did, she was to discover just how far and where his thoughts had travelled.

"I missed seeing him today."

"Yesterday, *mon chéri*. It is almost the dawn of a new day."

"Is it?" Roxton was surprised and fell silent.

She smiled into the cradle and sighed her contentment. Her sleeping son had nice rosy cheeks which told her he was in a deep sleep and had been for some time. She looked back at the Duke in profile.

"Did you rest at all in your closet?"

"No. There was no time. I go to Fontainebleau at first light."

This was news to Antonia. She did her best to sound disinterested.

"Will you be away for long?"

He looked at her then. "I do not want to be away from you, or him, at all. But I have some unfinished business to attend to. Two, maybe three nights at most."

She smiled up at him. "You must do what is necessary. We will miss you—but it can't be helped."

Her unswerving confidence was meant to help ease not add to the burden of whatever was troubling him. To her great surprise it instead unleashed in him a torrent of suppressed feeling, made all the more harrowing that he spoke in a harsh whisper in an attempt to keep his voice low, so as not to wake their son.

"I won't allow his life to be plagued by my follies! Julian is my son and heir. You are my wife—*my life*—and that is the beginning and the end to the matter!"

"As you are ours, *mon amour*. No one disputes that surely?"

"If I were to die today or tomorrow, or ten years hence—while he is still in his minority—I pledge on my honor that he will never suffer the likes of the—*deprivation*s and-and—*doubts* that were inflicted upon me by the fourth duke."

"Why would he?" Antonia replied evenly, forcing the panic back down her throat. She wanted to step away from the cradle, fearing their conversation might wake their son, but she stayed perfectly still. "You are nothing like your *grand-père*. And I have told you before, I will never let you leave us—"

"He will have no horrific surprises," he stated, unaware he had cut her off, so determined was he to emphasise his point. "Or have cause to call into question the childhood he spent with his parents, to wonder if those happy years were all a boy's flight of fancy."

"Renard, what happened while you were in Paris?"

"Let me tell you how I learned of Levron's existence," he stated, ignoring her question. "No guesses for who opened my eyes! The fourth duke took great delight in telling me that I was not the apple of my father's eye, and never had been. He said that apple belonged to another—to a *damned French bastard,* were his words. To prove his point, he showed me my father's last will and testament. And there in ink was a name I knew well. But next to that name were words that made no sense to me. Naturally I disbelieved what I read. The words… It said—*who I hereby lovingly acknowledge is my natural son.* I was made to repeat the name and that phrase, and then to write it out a hundred times so I never forgot that my father had another son, and one whom I was made to believe he loved more than he did me—"

"*Oh mon cœur,* to do that to a child—a child grieving the loss of his father—to make him question his father's love for him—it is terrible beyond words."

The Duke's gaze wandered back to the occupant of the cradle.

"Yes. The eleven-year-old boy adored his father; with his death he lost the centre of his world. The revelation of Levron's parentage was-was—*excruciating.* And for a short while the fourth duke achieved his object of tearing a rent in what should be an indissoluble bond between father and son, a bond he never had with his son. But I could not, and I do not denounce my father for not telling me that the shy young man who worked in our library was his natural son. I like to think that had my father lived he would have told me eventually—when I was old enough to understand the world and its—er—complexities. But to the fourth duke, Levron's existence was another weapon to add to his arsenal of hate he used to bend me to his will."

He shifted his gaze from his son to his wife.

"Antonia, nothing and no one must come between Julian and me. And I will take whatever steps are necessary to ensure our bond can *never* be severed."

She touched his cheek. "I believe you, *mon chéri*. And I know that you will. But Julian he will never experience what you did at the hands of your *grand-père*. The fourth duke was truly a monster who walked the surface of this earth, but he was also an aberration… Monseigneur," she added, a sudden flash of memory of a conversation they'd had the day they were married making her wonder if it might have a bearing on her duke's present preoccupation, which she still found mystifying. "Do you remember when you told me that you made no apologies for the way you had lived before we fell in love?"

"I do. But my life—*our life*—it is different now."

"Different because we now have Julian, yes?"

"Now we are married and yes, have a son. I own to conducting my past life as I saw fit and with little thought to the consequences on others." He smiled crookedly. "But marriage and fatherhood have a way of putting the past into perspective. I see now that certain particulars of the latter were effected under an assumption of naïve hubris."

"Renard, I do not worry about your past. It is done. All that matters is your present and your future—with *me*."

"Well said, *mignonne*."

He pulled her into his arms, and with her curves against him he breathed in the scent of her hair and it quietened his heart. He closed his eyes and dipped to whisper near her ear.

"I love you, *ma petite conseillère*."

"And I you, with all my heart, *l'amour de ma vie*."

They shared a gentle lingering kiss and then were content to remain still and silent in each other's arms, enjoying the moment and the quiet all around them. But when Antonia moved time on by taking a step back, the Duke let her go. She looked up at him with a crease between her brows.

"Renard, I said to you once that I would always prefer the truth, however much that truth might hurt me. I still believe that. I want you to always tell me the truth. I want you to tell me what happened in Paris when you visited Estée—"

"*Mignonne*, do not ask that of me now. When I return from Fontainebleau—"

"What is it that prevents you from telling me before you leave?"

"I will have a clearer idea of what I am up against after I visit Fontainebleau."

Antonia put her palm flat to the front of his silk banyan where she could feel the strong beating of his heart through his hard chest, and smiled up at him. "You may, that is true, but I will not, *mon mari chéri*. I am left here to worry and to speculate what it is that is weighing so heavily in here—on your heart. Why is it you cannot tell your wife what is bothering you so? And if you leave me guessing, and then—*À Dieu ne plaise!*—something were to happen to you? *You* would never forgive *yourself*. Eternity is a very long time to harbor regret—for you to wish you had confided in me, yes?"

His face split into a grin and he caught up her fingers to press his lips to the center of her palm. "You always have a wonderful way of putting everything into perspective, *ma fée*."

"I do! So tell me."

He lost his smile and looked into her clear green eyes, and there was such a depth of feeling in his dark gaze that she dared not breathe. And when he spoke the words were rasped out.

"I am told the Comtesse Duras-Valfons was safely delivered of a healthy son in the early Spring."

Antonia frowned in puzzlement, but when the Duke offered

nothing further, she cast her mind back to when she was first at Versailles living with her grandfather, and where she had often seen the Duke in company with the beautiful and statuesque Comtesse, she who was at that time his most recent mistress. And with a picture of the Comtesse hanging on the arm of her lover duke in her mind's eye, her head filled with dates and numbers and calculations. Those calculations came crashing together like two black clouds in a thunderstorm to form one possibility. She drew in a sharp breath of realisation, throat burning raw and dry.

"Her infant he is yours." It was not a question.

"That is what is being claimed, and why I ride to Fontainebleau."

"What do you intend to do?"

"To uphold my honor and protect my family? Whatever it takes."

"Yes of course. But the infant. He is an innocent. What do you intend to do about him?"

"If the Comtesse's claim proves to be true...? I have not the faintest idea. And *that* is the truth."

ELEVEN

A n invitation for Mme la Duchesse d'Roxton to attend a *soirée* at the Versailles home of the Marquise du Touraine-Brissac—the ancient aunt known as *Tante Philippe*—was delivered by liveried courier several hours after the Duke of Roxton's departure for Fontainebleau. The letter accompanying the invitation explained that the impromptu gathering was for family members arriving from Paris for the court's return to the palace.

Tante Philippe apologized for not giving Mme la Duchesse more time to organize her social obligations and would understand if she had already made other arrangements for the evening. Yet she sincerely hoped her nephew's wife could squeeze in a visit to her Salvan relations, who were all eager to make her reacquaintance before their court obligations intruded on their free time.

O ne of her ladies had come bustling into the noisy Gallery with the invitation while Antonia was at the far end, away from the ever-lively nursery, in the midst of the rehearsal for her court presentation, the dancing and protocol master M'sieur Beauchamp looking on with a critical eye.

The Duchess was making her exacting curtsey to Martin, who as the Queen of France was dutifully fluttering his fan and appearing regal, while Lord Vallentine had his chin in the air and was being suitably aloof as the King of France, elbow up on the mantel, a lace-bordered handkerchief in one limp hand.

Not wanting to lose her concentration and make a mistake, which would mean M'sieur Beauchamp making her start the ritual all over again, Antonia told her maid to give the invitation to His Majesty to open and read. And when the woman just stood there not understanding, His Lordship rolled his eyes and impatiently blurted out that he was Louis King of France and to be quick about it! He swiped the invitation and letter off the salver and with an impatient imperial wave worthy of a Bourbon king, sent the startled maid on her way, saying if there was a courier wanting a reply, he would have to await Louis' pleasure!

Relieved to finally have an excuse to lower his chin, His Lordship was also glad of the diversion. Being King of France was a fatiguing business.

He recognised the House of Touraine-Brissac's coat of arms on the black seals of both invitation and letter, being well-acquainted with all the ancient aunts and their progeny through his wife's interactions with her Salvan relatives, in writing and in person. He had reluctantly accompanied her to many a Salvan family *soirée*, never finding an adequate excuse to decline such events. So an invitation for Antonia to attend just such a gathering should have been a commonplace thing, and aside from the sheer relief of it not being for him there was no reason for him to think anything of it. But it bothered him, and made him suspicious, and for two reasons.

Of all the times he had visited the ancient aunts, he had never known *Tante Philippe* to host a family get-together. She left those to her sister the Comtesse du Chavigny—*Tante Victoire*. Everyone in the Salvan family was painfully aware of *Tante Philippe*'s parsimony. The family jest was that if she could get away with it *Tante Philippe* would have her servants pay their own way all for the privilege of serving her. The sad rumor was that her most devoted servants were owed more than a year's wages, and clung to their positions in the hopes of one day being paid. She did not discriminate. She had the same opinion and treated accordingly tradesmen, merchants, milliners, and her personal physician.

What else bothered Lord Vallentine about this particular invitation was the timing of its arrival, mere hours after the Duke had departed for Fontainebleau on business—the first night he was to spend away from his wife and son. He wouldn't put it past any of the ancient aunts to issue an invitation to the Duchess with the Duke's absence in mind. They had possibly been waiting for just such an opportunity so they could have the Duchess all to themselves without enduring the presence of her duke. Roxton always had a way of irritating his Salvan relatives, and with the banishment of the Comte de Salvan, interactions between nephew and ancient aunts had become strained, to say the least!

If it were up to him, he'd toss *Tante Philippe*'s invitation in the grate and be done with it. He was very sure the Duke would thank him for it. But he happened to look across at Antonia then and had a change of heart. She was all concentration in perfecting her exit from the presence of Her Majesty, slowly gliding backwards while kicking out the train of her gown with her heel, so as not to trip over her feet and the gown. It was an exacting—and to Vallentine—ludicrous piece of theater that required those being presented to have eyes in the back of their head. And it was made all the more fretfully hazardous with the entire court looking on, and most hoping for some failure or fall.

He wouldn't put his wife through such an ordeal for all the coffee in Persia!

And while it wasn't his place to comment or to wonder why Roxton was determined to have his duchess go through with a court presentation, it did worry him that she was spending an inordinate amount of time being studious. And when she wasn't involved in the exacting lessons of court deportment under M'sieur Beauchamp's critical eye, she was mothering a ducal infant, not to mention the constant demands of running a household. When, to his way of thinking, what she ought to be doing was enjoying life. It was the Duke who had reminded him that at the same age as his duchess they were a couple of Merry-Andrews with not a care in the world. She needed time away—a distraction —from all this pompous protocol and mothering mayhem.

His choice was clear.

He would sacrifice himself on the high altar of family duty, forfeit a quiet evening at home perusing the latest English newssheets, and accompany his sister-in-law to the *soirée* at the Hôtel Touraine-Brissac. It was the least he could do. Besides, she couldn't very well go alone. He had sworn an oath to his best friend to protect and keep her and his little lordship safe whenever Roxton was away from home. But he wasn't about to make this sacrifice alone. If he had to commit to an evening in the company of the ancient aunts, and without his wife there to shield him from their spidery web of intrigue, then he needed a second.

"You're comin' with us," he stated to Martin Ellicott, five minutes after handing over the invitation while they were sitting in the orangery enjoying coffee and gateaux in the winter sunshine. "No argument."

Antonia looked up from *Tante Philippe's* letter with a bright smile. She had changed out of her court gown and over-sized panniers and was wearing a floral silk caraco jacket and pink silk quilted petticoat. "Oh! That is an excellent idea, Lucian. Martin, say you will attend!"

"I was not about to refuse, Mme la Duchesse," Martin replied inclining his head, a side-long look at His Lordship. "It would be my honor, and also my first official engagement in my new—um —circumstances"

"Don't get too enthused," Vallentine threw at him, reaching for another *pâte à choux*. He bit into the small cream-filled pastry. "*Tante Philippe* is a notorious penny-father. Can't prise a *sou* out of her fist! So don't expect much in the way of refreshment or entertainment. Though," he mused, licking his lips free of cream, "as this is your first time in their company, you probably will be amused." He pulled his long frame up to sit higher in the chair, adding with a weary sigh, "Their appeal wears thin quickly, let me tell you. And I wouldn't apportion blame if you were to escape the salon and join me at the bottom of the garden." He grinned sheepishly. "That's where I'll be and where I head at the first opportunity, and where I stay, mindin' my own business until called to say m' farewells. Estée hardly notices I've been missin'."

"Lucian, I do not know if I can accept," Antonia announced, putting aside the invitation and letter near her porcelain coffee dish. "It is this evening, so there is no time for me to send to the *hôtel* for one of my gowns. All I brought with me from Paris are these plain clothes—"

"*Plain?*" Lord Vallentine gave a snort. "There's nothin' plain about 'em! They're very fetchin', and no one would say otherwise. You could wear what you've got on now and not one Salvan relative would blink a jaundiced eyelid. Though the ancient aunts will turn a greenish shade of envy that Roxton spares no expense on your wardrobe."

"His Lordship is correct, Mme la Duchesse," Martin agreed. "Your caraco and petticoat would not be out of place in any salon, particularly as this invitation says the *soirée* is to be a family affair—"

Vallentine snapped his fingers. "That's right! Ellicott has hit on the proverbial! As it's just to be family present, I doubt the ancient aunts will have their jewelry dug out of the vault, and they certainly won't waste coin on new petticoats just to impress each other. Remember what I said about *Tante Philippe's* tight fists."

"I do not forget, Lucian, but have *you* forgotten that the court it continues to mourn for the Dauphine?" Antonia argued. "And until *Sa Majesté* says otherwise, everyone must wear black, and all the time. The whole of the town—shops, carriages, even the sedans—they are all draped in mourning. Surely you have seen this on your way to and from *La Grande Écurie*. It is very drab. But M'sieur le Duc says we do not need to wear mourning while we are at home. It is only when I venture from the house, and of course for my presentation. So perhaps it will be the same with this *soirée*, because although it is venturing out, we are visiting family?" She sighed. "I wish Monseigneur he were here to advise me. He would know."

Vallentine didn't say so, but he doubted very much there would have been an invitation to the Salvan *soirée* had the Duke been at home.

"You may well be right," His Lordship offered, "but by my reckonin', as *Tante Philippe* is a notorious penny pincher, and her sisters have less than a full purse of coins between them, they'll have limited the expense of their black garb to what is most necessary. And they won't waste wearin' their mournin' gowns if only family are present. Why would they? They're not venturin' out. And who wouldn't want to wear somethin' other than black in my own home, and leave the drabs for when out in the public eye. What think you, Ellicott? Seem reasonable?"

"It does, my lord. Mme du Touraine-Brissac states in her invitation that it is an impromptu gathering. That leads one to believe invitations to other family members were also sent out late. I should think then that those who do attend will wear whatever they have to hand, and are used to wearing in each other's company."

"There! Couldn't have said it better myself. Though I think I did say that? No matter! What matters is that you'd best wear somethin' summerish—"

"In autumn?" Antonia was aghast. "So you have a reason to

wear black, too, when I catch my death by cold? It is almost cold enough to freeze the pond water!"

"But you wear summer garments here in the villa—"

"Have you not noticed we have *four* Dutch heaters, and so," Antonia added with a beaming smile, "it is always summer indoors."

"Aha! But what you don't know, *chère belle-sœur*, is that while you can't prize a denier out of *Tante Philippe*, she spares no expense on fuel for her fires. Keeps her rooms warmer than a bedpan full of hot coals!" He frowned and mused, "Must be a Salvan trait Roxton picked up too, this need for over-heated housin'." He leaned forward and looked from Antonia to Martin, and lowered his voice. "Word is, she's preparin' for the afterlife."

"By keeping her rooms heated?" Martin Ellicott interrupted in some surprise, a side-long glance at the Duchess who was staring at His Lordship with the same amount of puzzlement. "How —extraordinary!"

Vallentine kept his features neutral, adding in the same whispered aside, "Not when you know her afterlife is going to be spent —" He pointed to the flagstones. "—down there, because she won't be welcome—" He pointed skywards. "—up there."

Antonia and Martin burst out laughing.

TWELVE

ANY MISGIVINGS Lord Vallentine had about the timing of the invitation to the Salvan *soirée* while the Duke was away evaporated watching Antonia descend the main staircase. He had one word for how she looked, and he found himself using it often where his sister-in-law was concerned: breathtaking.

It was obvious she had taken great care to choose an outfit that was understated, yet the choice of fabrics and decoration proclaimed her rank as the wife of the preeminent nobleman in the United Kingdom. Her *Pet-en-l'air* jacket of shimmering ivory silk brocade was richly embroidered with sprays of colorful flowers on large cuffed sleeves, back pleats and side skirts. A lace-edged gossamer fichu, criss-crossed over her ample bosom, was tucked into the low square-cut décolletage. The side skirts of this sack-backed jacket flared out over a hooped gown of palest green silk that had but one ruche border at its hem.

The silk mules on her stockinged feet were in a matching fabric and embroidery to her jacket, and with a two-inch heel helped compensate for her diminutive stature. As for accessories, a gouache-painted fan dangled from a gloved wrist, and a single strand of pearls encircled her throat. Her honey hair was simply dressed in a multitude of braids threaded with satin ribbons the same shade of green as her silk petticoat, wound close to her head and held in place by many pins. One aigrette hair comb above her left ear was smothered in tiny diamonds which sparkled in the candlelight.

Martin Ellicott, who was at Lord Vallentine's shoulder and also had his chin tilted up to admire the Duchess on her descent, voiced what they were both thinking, saying on a sigh of happiness, "None rival her beauty…"

"With her face and figure she could turn a gunny sack into the height of fashion!" Vallentine said under his breath with a huff, and tore his gaze away when a solicitous footman stepped forward and offered him his sword and belt. He continued in an under-voice. "*Psst. Ellicott.* We need to keep on the alert tonight! I don't trust those Salvan sisters. That invitation got me thinkin' while I was dressin'. And I wouldn't put it past the ancient aunts to have orchestrated this family gatherin' just so *she* can make Montbelliard's acquaintance without the Duke present—"

"—because he failed in his bid to do so here?" Martin was surprised but not shocked. "I take your point, and accept we need to be cautious. M'sieur le Duc will not be happy—"

"He'll be livid. But we can't not attend now. She's lookin' forward to it. But we can limit the damage, by makin' certain one of us never leaves her side, eh?"

"Of course, my lord. That is wise—Mme la Duchesse!" Martin said aloud, breaking off his under-voiced conversation with Lord Vallentine because Antonia had come straight up to them. "As always you are beauty personified. And the pearls are a wise choice for a family gathering. M'sieur le Duc would certainly approve."

Antonia looked at Vallentine and then back at Martin, and was unconvinced.

"You are talking about something else entirely, Lucian's face it says so. But you can tell me about that later. For now, we concentrate on our little excursion to the ancient aunts. And so, merci, Martin. My women they tried to have me wear all sorts of jewelry pieces, but I said no. I do not want to make the ancient aunts uncomfortable by putting under their noses Monseigneur's great wealth. He is very generous to me, and if he were here, I would wear one or two more pieces to please him. But sadly, he is not…" She sighed deeply. "I miss him, and more so tonight…" She forced herself to smile. "And so I wear only the pearls."

Martin stepped aside to allow the butler to help Antonia into a fur-lined velvet cloak, while His Lordship went to the long looking glass in the corner of the foyer to adjust his sword and belt to his satisfaction. Meanwhile, Antonia's lady-in-waiting Gabrielle, who was already in her cloak and carrying the Duchess's fur muff, went straight out to the carriage under the *porte-cochère* to ensure all was in readiness for her mistress.

"There's a hot brick in the carriage for y'feet," Vallentine informed Antonia as he was shrugged into a scarlet-lined roquelaure. "I don't want Roxton blamin' me for turnin' your toes blue."

"It is not my toes which will be of concern but the tip of my nose! Now please, we must hurry. I do not wish to be late," she threw over her shoulder as she followed Gabrielle out to the carriage on the arm of Martin Ellicott.

"It's fashionable to be late, y'know!" Vallentine argued, climbing up into the velvet upholstered interior of the Duke of Roxton's second-best carriage to sit next to Martin Ellicott. "Roxton makes a point of bein' late for every event he ever attends."

"He does. And he always makes a splendid entrance," Antonia said with pride, and looked to Martin. "One day—soon I hope— you will finally see just how splendid is Monseigneur's arrival, and how he plays to his audience. He is *éblouissant*."

"I look forward to the day, Mme la Duchesse," Martin Ellicott replied. "I confess that over the years I have often wished to see the result of the small part I played in his sartorial splendor."

"Well, I wish he were here now so you could, Ellicott," said Lord Vallentine, and knocked on the headboard with his knuckle, signal for the driver to set to. He settled his straight shoulders against the padded upholstery and frowned at Antonia. "You never did say why he had to gallop off to Fontainebleau."

"I did not. But perhaps I can remember why if you tell me what the two of you were whispering about in the foyer as I came down the stairs?"

When Vallentine and Martin Ellicott glanced at one another without daring to change their expressions, mouths shut tight, she giggled behind her gloved hand.

"Aha! As that is how it is, you will allow me to look out the window and ask me no more questions about M'sieur le Duc."

THE CARRIAGE RIDE to the hôtel Touraine on the rue de la Paroisse was of short duration. The Villa Roxton in its expansive garden and backing on to the royal parkland might be on the outskirts of the new town, but the planned township was not much bigger than a large village, and so getting from place to place took no time at all. In fact, Antonia could have easily been transported to her destination in her birthday sedan chair. But that would have meant His Lordship and Martin Ellicott going on foot or horseback beside her, and leaving Gabrielle at the villa.

Lord Vallentine insisted she bring at least one of her women along, and as it was an evening affair with the hours of daylight getting shorter, he wasn't taking the risk of returning to the villa in the dark without an escort. Roxton would never forgive him if they were held up, or some mishap befell her sedan chair in the dark. The only way to travel then was by carriage.

Antonia considered it excessive to have liveried postilions accompany the carriage front and back, but again Vallentine would not brook any opposition, saying it was what Roxton would expect. He got no argument from her. She was too excited to be going out for the evening that she was happy with whatever arrangements were decided on her behalf.

It was not many minutes before the ducal procession left the rue des Reservoirs and turned into the rue de la Paroisse. A much narrower street, lined either side with cream-colored villas with blue-painted shutters and doors, it was congested with carriages and sedan chairs as far as the eye could see. This considerably slowed the progress of the ducal carriage, and had Antonia peering out the window wondering if there had been an accident.

And when the carriage came to a complete standstill, His Lordship pushed down the sash and stuck his powdered head out of the window. He shouted at one of the postilions to go on ahead and find out what all the fuss was about.

He then put up the sash against the cold, and threw himself back against the upholstery.

"Y'think this lot could coordinate their social calendars so their *soirées* were held on different evenin's! But no! Got to outdo each other on the same night."

"With the court returning from Fontainebleau at the end of the week," Martin commented, "it seems the courtiers are determined to enjoy their last days of freedom before they resume their duties."

"Duties? Pah! Bein' a courtier must be a ghastly tedious business," Lord Vallentine opined, screwing up his face as if he had tasted something sour. "Standin' about all day just so you can hand a glove, or a handkerchief, or a plate of-of *eels*, to the next chap, who then passes it on the next fellow of a higher rank, and so forth and so on, until it reaches His Majesty is beyond idiocy in my considered opinion."

"But, my lord, surely our French cousins feel amply rewarded by the honor done them in handling the royal glove or that—um —plate of eels?" Martin remarked with a flicker of a smile. "Not everyone is so privileged—"

"Rewarded? Privileged? Ha!" Vallentine spat out, rising to the bait. "Not in my books it ain't! And I don't care who hears it—it's a lot of sycophantic nonsense that no Englishman would stand for at the court of St. James's. Give me a German George who knows his place and takes the advice of his ministers. Not a bunch of prancin' perfumed fopdoodles—"

"—carrying a plate of eels?" Martin interjected lightly.

"Lucian, are you calling Monseigneur a fopdoodle?" Antonia demanded, turning her gaze away from the view of the same villa, the carriage at a complete standstill, to raise her arched brows at her brother-in-law.

"Eh? Wh-what? No! No! A'course not! I wasn't referrin' to—Damme! Now you're both laughin' at me."

Antonia shook her head and hid her giggling behind her fluttering fan, but there was no hiding the merriment in her green eyes. Finally she brought herself under control and said solemnly, "That was *très méchant* of me and so I apologise." She asked, "Lucian, have you considered that all the people in these carriages may be attending the same *soirée*, and at a *hôtel* in this street or in one close by, and it is the ancient aunts who have scheduled their *soirée* at the same time as this other event?"

Lord Vallentine gave a start, as if this had never occurred to him and then he let out a bark of laughter. "Haha! Yes! And m' money is on *Tante Philippe* not gettin' an invite to this other *rassemblement*, so in a fit of pique she's holdin' one of her own. That would account for the short notice and her openin' her fists to fund her own revelry."

"*Voilà pourquoi.* Then this mystery it solves itself," Antonia announced, and flashing a cheeky smile at Martin, she said to His Lordship on a sigh, "And now we can look forward to a dull evening with the fopdoodles of the court."

THIRTEEN

WHEN THE OCCUPANTS of M'sieur le Duc d'Roxton's second-best carriage finally alighted under the *porte-cochère* of the hôtel Touraine, they were greeted by a contingent of footmen attired not in the customary livery of the noble household but dressed entirely in black. This was not surprising, given the whole town was in mourning, but something about their harried expressions bothered Lord Vallentine.

In fact, the unusual amount of traffic encountered in this street had fuelled his misgivings. The comings and goings of carriages and sedan chairs was extraordinary. And turning in under the *porte-cochère* he also noticed a large contingent of chairmen loitering nearby. It made him wonder if they were not the only guests at this *soirée*—that it was entirely probable that the event the Duchess had spoken about which might also be occurring in this street was in fact happening under this very roof!

The porter's furtive glances while they were shrugged out of their cloaks and coats only increased these suspicions.

For His Lordship it all added up to this *soirée* smelling off— like a haddock left out in the noonday sun. It might look fine from a distance, but the closer one got the smellier it became. His anxiety led him to offer Antonia reassurance, which only put her on the alert and made Martin Ellicott wonder further what was actually going on.

Stooping to the Duchess's ear as they ascended the grand staircase behind the butler, he was heard to hiss loudly, "Just cause the servants are in liveried mourning don't mean the rest of the family will be wearing their black."

But they were. All ten of them.

THE ANCIENT AUNTS and their family members had positioned themselves under a central chandelier in the second of two salons, with the ladies on stiff-backed chairs, and the gentlemen standing behind. They looked to be arranged for the painting of a family portrait, but the requisite painter with his easel was nowhere to be found.

Not only were the women's gowns of black wool but the lace at their elbows, their folding fans, stockings, and hair ribbons, were also black, and any jewelry was of jet. The gentlemen, too, wore black wool ensembles, with the buttons of waistcoat and frock coat covered in matching black fabric. Their cravats were of black silk, as were their pocket handkerchiefs, and the satin ribbons in their hair.

Had they not been under the chandelier's glow, Antonia would have found it difficult to see them at all, for the walls between the tall windows were also draped in wide lengths of black cloth, and the curtains of black velvet were pulled on the fading afternoon light. But she could not miss their expressions in the candlelight. Regardless of age, everyone from sixteen to sixty was grim-faced

The butler stopped at the entrance to the larger salon and announced the newest arrivals, and all the women, even the elderly, rose as one, but everyone remained where they were, and their expressions did not change.

Before they had reached the second salon, Lord Vallentine caught at Antonia's cuffed sleeve. He could barely contain his rage.

"Let me deal with this-this—*ambuscade*," he enunciated through gritted teeth.

"No, Lucian," Antonia said under her breath. "We must not let them see that it bothers us—"

Vallentine did not wait to hear the rest of her objection. He was too angry. He strode into the second salon, Martin Ellicott mechanically following on his heels. Antonia would have followed too except she was distracted by the loud hissing of her name, which made her pause and look over her shoulder. And there, in a far corner, head poking out from behind a jib door in the wall panelling, was her lady-in-waiting Gabrielle.

"Mme la Duchesse! Come! Please! Come this way!"

Antonia hovered in surprised indecision. So Gabrielle implored again, this time beckoning with a hand gesture that could not be misinterpreted—the Duchess was to be quick about it.

Curious, Antonia crossed over to the jib door to ask what Gabrielle was doing back there when the door was thrust wide.

"Forgive me, Mme la Duchesse. It cannot be helped."

And with that pronouncement, Gabrielle grabbed her mistress about the wrist and pulled her through the opening. As she did so, someone brushed past Antonia in the opposite direction, out into the salon. The jib door was shut tight and vanished into the wall panelling once again. To anyone in the salon, it was as if the Duchess had disappeared.

On the other side of the door, Antonia and Gabrielle were in darkness. But they were not alone.

FOURTEEN

A SINGLE FLICKERING candle hovered just out of reach of Antonia's toes on the narrow landing of a tight spiral staircase. As her sight adjusted to the darkness, a mature woman's face came into view in the candle's pale yellow glow. She looked familiar. And yet Antonia knew she was a stranger.

"We must hurry, Mme la Duchesse," she hissed. "Sophie will say you are indisposed, but she cannot hold them off forever. Come!"

When Antonia hesitated, Gabrielle whispered near her ear, "You can trust this woman. She is my sister Giselle. Please, Mme la Duchesse. All will become clear. I promise you."

If Antonia had a moment of panic, it evaporated on the reassurances of her most trusted and fiercely devoted maid. Without further ado, she lifted the hem of her silk petticoats and carefully and calmly followed Gabrielle's sister Giselle down the winding stair to an entresol.

The low-ceiled *petit apartment* had sparse furnishings, and set in a row of archways were small windows through which filtered wintery daylight. Without a fire and no heating to this part of the house, it was cold and dank. Giselle continued through to a second room, where several but not all the candles in the sconces were lit. A curtained bed was tucked into an alcove, and two chairs and a small worktable were against one wall.

Antonia gave an involuntary shiver, her summery jacket and petticoats inadequate for an unheated room. But her curiosity as to why she was here, and interest in her surroundings, made her dismiss her own discomfort and look about. She wondered if she was to sit on one of these chairs, when a young woman about her own age and dressed all in black came bustling through from a third connecting room.

"For-forgive our duplicity, Mme la Duchesse!" the young woman announced breathlessly, as if she had run all the way. She dropped into a deep curtsey. "But I had—I had to speak with you because my *Grand-mère* she is determined to marry me to a man who is a widower twice over. But it is Hubert I love. *Grand-mère* refuses to listen. And my father he says I cannot marry Hubert while his prospects are in-in *limbo*—which I do not understand at all because one day Hubert will be a comte. It's just that it is not today or tomorrow, so it is not soon enough for my grandmother or my father!"

"I am very sorry for your difficulties," Antonia said evenly, trying to make sense of the young woman's verbal assault, and acutely aware that she had in effect been abducted by these women. "But none of what you say answers why I am here and what you expect of me. I do not even know your name! Though your blue eyes tell me you are a Salvan, yes?"

"Forgive me, Mme la Duchesse. I am Elisabeth-Louise Salvan Gondi Touraine—youngest daughter of the Duc du Touraine who is son of Mme Touraine-Brissac—"

"*Tante Philippe* she is your *Grand-mère*?"

"Regrettably so, Mme la Duchesse. My father has given me into her care, and she is nothing but a-a—*tyrant*—"

"Mlle Elisabeth-Louise!" Gabrielle's sister Giselle chastised.

"Mme la Duchesse will gain the wrong impression of *you* if you make impolite remarks about Mme la Marquise du Touraine-Brissac."

Elisabeth-Louise ignored her maid, explaining to Antonia with a sad twisted smile, "I truly believe my *Grand-mère* wishes my life to be miserable because everything about me offends her."

"I have one of those grandmothers, too," Antonia replied with a sympathetic smile. "What is it you want of me?"

"Mme la Duchesse, I beg you—Hubert begs you—*we* petition you—to speak with M'sieur le Duc on our behalf. Hubert he has applied many times for an interview but to no avail. All he requires is five minutes of M'sieur le Duc d'Roxton's time. And I know my father would listen to M'sieur le Duc. They are cousins and good friends, and if M'sieur le Duc had no objection to our marriage, then *Grand-mère* she cannot object, and—"

Antonia took a step closer, peering keenly at Elisabeth-Louise.

"Mlle Touraine, we have only just met, and in the most star-tling way, and you expect me to plead your case to M'sieur le Duc? I only have your word, but perhaps your father and grandmother have good reason to object to the match? Nor do I know the first thing about your qualities, or the qualities of the man whom you wish to marry. I would not blame M'sieur le Duc for thinking his wife she had drunk a little too much wine were I to go to him with nothing more than your name and wish to marry this Hubert."

"Ah, Mme la Duchesse! But you married M'sieur le Duc for love!" Elisabeth-Louise declared. "*Grand-mère* says love matches are for the *paysannerie,* and not for our kind. She says your marriage is a peculiarity that has done our families a disservice because it has given daughters of the *noblesse d'épée* such as me false hope that we too can marry for love! I tell you in all honesty, Mme la Duchesse, that my grandmother is still in a state of shock that the great satyr duke was brought to his knees and made a love match. But I do not care how astonished or disgruntled she is, because I believe we should be able to marry for love, too. *You* are the example and your marriage gives Hubert and me such hope."

"I am flattered, *ma chère fille*," Antonia replied gently, and shivered, the cold seeping through her light clothing. "But you are greatly mistaken if you think that because M'sieur le Duc he loves me it has dulled his faculties in any way. He remains M'sieur le Duc d'Roxton, and he stands tall on his two feet, and always will. I am very sorry, but if your father and your grandmother are not for a marriage with this Hubert, then M'sieur le Duc he will not interfere, with or without my pleas on your behalf—"

"But Mme la Duchesse, it is because of *you* that my grandmother objects to my marriage."

"*Pourquoi*? Because M'sieur le Duc he fell in love with me?"

"No, Mme la Duchesse. But because you are blamed for our cousin the Comte de Salvan being stripped of his offices of state and banished from court. And now we Salvans are burdened with his disgrace, and the ancient aunts who lived off his charity are even poorer than—"

Antonia turned to her maid. "I do not understand at all why you have brought me here to be insulted in this way!"

"Mme la Duchesse, I would never have agreed to this meeting had I known Mlle Touraine's true intentions," Gabrielle whispered fiercely. "I am as surprised as you. Giselle she told me—"

"Mme la Duchesse! Elisabeth-Louise's intentions are wholly her own!" Giselle interrupted. "She was to confide in you something else entirely, and if there were a moment to plead her case about her own difficulties, to do so after you were made aware of certain-certain—*particular*s occurring in this house at this very moment."

"Mme la Duchesse, you must believe us!" Gabrielle beseeched.

"I do. But I am cold, and we are leaving. Before I do," Antonia added, fixing her green eyes on Elisabeth-Louise and squaring her shoulders. "I must dismiss a mistruth: M'sieur le Comte de Salvan was poor before his banishment, and sought to relieve his financial troubles by contracting a marriage with me, against my will, but with the connivance of the ancient aunts. There is a great deal more but it is too painful for me to recount. I forgive you your great ignorance because you have been told falsehoods. And now you will return me to where it is warm, and to M'sieur Vallentine, who I am very sure is tearing this house apart in search of me. *Soyez rapide à ce sujet!*"

To everyone's astonishment, Elisabeth-Louise fell to her knees and snatched up the hem of the Duchess's silk petticoat and pressed it to her damp cheek, making it impossible for Antonia to move.

"Please! Mme la Duchesse! I beg you! I may never have another opportunity, and you may never talk to me again, if that is your wish, but I need you to hear what I have to say!"

"Elisabeth-Louise! Get up!" Giselle demanded in an embarrassed whisper, grabbing her young mistress by the upper arm and trying to haul her to her feet. "You are making a fool of yourself, and you are embarrassing Mme la Duchesse! This is no way to seek help—"

"No! Do not touch me! You do not know! No one knows! Not even Hubert knows! If Mme la Duchesse cannot help me, then I am ruined and forever damned!"

The girl then burst into sobs, and remained prostrate at Antonia's feet, still clutching at the hem of her petticoat, as if needing anchorage. Regarding her, Antonia had a stab of acuity so keen it brought back memories of her own sad predicament when she was living with her grandmother, desperately in love with the Duke, yet unsure of her future. She was so despairing of her dire situation that she had made plans to run away to Venice.

"Giselle, fetch your mistress a cordial," she ordered quietly. "Gabrielle, give your handkerchief to Mlle Touraine, and help her to a chair. Then bring me the coverlet off that bed. I am chilled to the bone. If there is another, use it yourself."

With the girl's maid gone from the room and Elisabeth-Louise

seated at the table, her damp face dried with Gabrielle's handkerchief, Antonia sat opposite her, wrapped in the bed quilt, and said,

"Mlle, if you want my help, you must tell me the truth."

Elisabeth-Louise sniffed and nodded eagerly. "Yes, Mme la
Duchesse. Ask me anything!"

"You are *enceinte*, yes?"

The gasp came not from the girl, but from Gabrielle.

FIFTEEN

E LISABETH-LOUISE burst into fresh tears at Antonia's gentle but blunt question, so there was no need to seek further confirmation. As Giselle was to return at any moment with the cordial, Antonia pressed upon the girl to confide her predicament without embellishment. Only in this way could Antonia determine what help she could offer. And with such a willing ear and sympathetic audience Elisabeth-Louise needed no encouragement.

Hubert had been courting her for months without her family —particularly her grandmother—being aware of their feelings for one another. He was a regular visitor, often accompanying his mentor, the Marquis de Chesnay. But it only became apparent why the Marquis was visiting so often when he announced to her grandmother that he wished to make Elisabeth-Louise his third wife. Naturally the young couple were horrified at the prospect. That is when Hubert wrote to the Duc du Touraine seeking permission to wed his daughter. This alerted her grandmother to Hubert's intentions and Elisabeth-Louise was forbidden from seeing him again.

"We were forced to meet in secret, at the house of my sister

Michelle," Elisabeth-Louise explained. "Perhaps, Mme la Duchesse, you have heard my sister's three daughters playing out in their garden? Michelle lives in the house next to yours. And I have seen you, from the windows of her house, out in your garden with your women and your infant. Giselle has never said a word to our grandmother about my visits with Hubert at Michelle's house because it allows her to see *her* sisters, Michelle's maid Rose and your maid Gabrielle."

At this revelation, Antonia stopped her and stared at Gabrielle.

"It is true, Mme la Duchesse. And there is our fourth sister, Yvette, she is the eldest and personal maid to M'sieur le Duc's sister Mme Vallentine. I did tell you about Yvette, but not about Giselle and Rose."

"*Bon Dieu*! Are *all* your sisters maids in the houses of our relatives?"

"Yes, Mme la Duchesse," Gabrielle replied matter-of-factly. "How else do we find good positions in the best households if not through our family connections?"

"I knew all the noble families were related to one another by blood and marriage, but I admit to learning something new today!" Antonia smiled. "I had no notion that the smallness of our world it is the same for you, too. That is very pleasing, and I am glad you are able to see your sisters."

"Thank you, Mme la Duchesse," Gabrielle replied, returning the smile. "It is a small world for all of us. For those of us who serve, as well as for those of you who are served. And that is also why it is no coincidence Mlle Touraine's sister lives in the house next to the villa because I was the one who told my sister Rose who told her mistress that the house it was for lease."

"Mme la Duchesse, please do not blame Hubert for-for my predicament," Elisabeth-Louise said in a small voice, lowering her lashes, cheeks glowing. "We are secretly betrothed, and we truly believed our marriage would be a mere formality. That is why I—he—*we*—allowed ourselves to-to—" She burst into fresh tears and covered her face before blurting out, "It happened only twice! We had meant to wait until after our vows but—"

"Please. No more. Dry your eyes, *ma chère fille*," Antonia said gently, adding with a little laugh, "Believe me, I am the last person who would blame you for succumbing to your desires. I am no hypocrite." She took a deep breath, adding matter-of-factly, "What is done is done, and now cannot be undone. What we must look to is your future and how I can best help you with the outcome you both desire, and as soon as possible."

Elisabeth-Louise's eyes shone. "You will speak with M'sieur le Duc? You will—"

"I will. Though that is all I can promise."

Elisabeth-Louise leapt off the chair, threw herself at Antonia's feet, and hugged her about the ankles. "Oh thank you! Thank you! You are too kind! Too generous!"

"Of a sudden I feel old," Antonia muttered, reluctantly removing her hand from the warmth amongst the folds of the bed quilt to give the girl an affectionate pat on the shoulder. "Gabrielle, help Mlle Touraine back to her chair."

When Elisabeth-Louise was once again still and quiet, Antonia said seriously, "Be aware that while I will do my very best to put your case to M'sieur le Duc, I will never ask him to act contrary to his honor. He will listen to me, but his decision is his to make. You understand?" When the girl nodded, she regarded her with a small, knowing smile. "I think you are smarter than you appear because not once have you mentioned Hubert's family name. And you did this deliberately, did you not, because you were afraid that if I knew from the outset that your Hubert is in fact the Chevalier Montbelliard I would not listen to you at all. So! No more playing games! I may be a little older than you—"

"I am twenty, Mme la Duchesse."

Antonia hardly missed a beat. "I may be a little younger than you, but that is of no matter. But tell me. I am curious. Why are you not married already? The daughters of the *noblesse d'épée* are married off well before your age, yes?"

"My sisters were fourteen when they married, that is true, Mme la Duchesse. I was betrothed, but he died when I was thirteen and then my father he left me at the *Abbaye-aux-Bois*. Perhaps because he had married my sister Michelle to Gerard, the son of a Farmer-General, against *Grand-mère*'s wishes. She has never forgiven him for bringing disgrace to our name—"

"Because your sister she was married off to one of the bourgeoisie?"

"Yes, Mme la Duchesse. And that is why my grandmother is determined to force me into a marriage with the Marquis de Chesnay. But I know once you have put my case to M'sieur le Duc, my grandmother will be forced to change her mind. Besides, she cannot truly object, when Hubert will one day be Comte de Salvan."

"I am sorry to say that exchanging suitors will not be as easy as you think," Antonia stated gently. "The Comte de Salvan is M'sieur le Duc's sworn enemy, and that is one big impediment for your happiness with the Chevalier Montbelliard." She stood, keeping the quilt wrapped about her, adding, "At least one mystery it is solved. I no longer need wonder why the Chevalier he was intent on making my acquaintance… He hoped, like you, to persuade me to speak to M'sieur le Duc on his behalf. But I presume the urgency of your situation is lost on your Hubert because you have yet to share with him your great surprise, yes? And why you took matters into your own hands and orchestrated this meeting to plead your case. And a success for you, too, as I have agreed to speak with M'sieur le Duc on your behalf. *Tiens voilà!*"

With Antonia up off the chair, Elisabeth-Louise was quick to scramble to her feet. She did not deny anything the Duchess had said. In fact, she was even more in awe of her, blurting out, "For one who is so very beautiful you are also very clever!"

"Beauty is no barrier to cleverness or stupidity, Mlle Touraine." Antonia's green eyes sparkled and she smiled cheekily. "But you are correct. I am clever. Which is why Monseigneur he loves me. And now I have spent long enough in this cold cellar of a room," she added flatly, unwrapping herself and handing the quilt to Gabrielle. "I must return before I am truly missed. Please show me to M'sieur Vallentine—"

Elisabeth-Louise moved into Antonia's path and bobbed another curtsey. "Forgive me for taking up your time with my concerns, Mme la Duchesse, but I need tell you something that is a concern to *you*. It is the reason you were brought here."

Antonia bit back a retort and tempered her impatience and said bluntly, "Tell me as succinctly as possible, before icicles they form on my arms."

"You were invited here under false pretences. Not only family members but all of society are assembled here tonight. Which is why I had to stop you entering *Grand-mère*'s salon. She knows M'sieur le Duc is out of town. She made certain he would be away so you would come alone." When Antonia said nothing and continued to stare at her, Elisabeth-Louise continued in hushed tones. "*Grand-mère* intends to announce her deep regret before all her guests as to M'sieur le Duc d'Roxton's absence. And then, Mme la Duchesse, she will ask you why he did not accompany you—"

"She is like my grandmother!" Antonia quipped.

"—knowing that he has gone to Fontainebleau, and why—"

"She knows M'sieur le Duc has gone to Fontainebleau—and-and *why*?" Antonia repeated in disbelief.

"They *all* know. *And* they know *why* he has gone there. She told them!"

Antonia was shaken to speechlessness by this revelation. She stared at the girl without seeing her, hard-gripping the closed sticks of her fan. And because she did not react, Elisabeth-Louise wondered if the Duchess disbelieved her, and so she elaborated.

"*Grand-mère* was all sympathy for you over her *café au lait*, saying we must do our best not to mention the fact that M'sieur le Duc had dashed off to Fontainebleau the moment the Comtesse Duras-Valfons beckoned him to her. That she did not mean to boast but she knew it was only a matter of time before M'sieur le Duc returned to his wicked satyr ways. She says a zebra cannot change its stripes, nor a silly little butterfly of a girl hope to hold the attentions of one who has spent a lifetime spreading the wings of hundreds of beauteous butterflies—"

"I have heard enough." Antonia's throat burned. "I do not know if I wish to thank you or scold you for repeating such spiteful nonsense. And now you will show me out of here. *Merci.*"

It was Gabrielle's turn to stop the Duchess from leaving.

"Mme la Duchesse, please. Mlle Touraine has more to tell—"

"More? There is more of this-this dross, this *méchante absurdité* for me to hear? No, Gabrielle," Antonia stated, and brushed past her, bustling back the way they had come, towards the spiral staircase. "No! No! No! I will not listen to another horrid word said about M'sieur le Duc—"

"The baby!" Gabrielle burst out, not knowing any other way of getting her mistress to stop and listen. "Mme la Duchesse—Mme Duras-Valfons' infant—it is *here*. Her *bébé* it is here in *this* house!"

WHEN GISELLE finally returned from the kitchens with the cordial, the entresol was empty. She checked all four rooms, and even went up the spiral stair to the jib door that opened into the second salon. Hearing raised voices, she rightly presumed the maid standing guard on the other side was now having difficulty convincing whoever was shouting at her that the Duchess remained indisposed after all this time.

She checked that the bolt securing the door against trespass was still fixed firmly in place, then retraced her steps and left the entresol. Confident she knew where Elisabeth-Louise had taken the Duchess, she traversed a labyrinth of tight servant passageways and draughty narrow backstairs until she arrived at a tiny attic room under the mansard roof in the farthest reaches of the hôtel. Here neither family, servant, nor guest would hear the discordant wailing of a neglected infant.

SIXTEEN

ALL OF SOCIETY was assembled in the Marquise du Touraine-Brissac's *salle de bal* under the bright candlelight of three chandeliers, and hundreds more candles in ornate mirrored wall sconces. At any other time, the guests in metallic thread embroidered silks and glittering jewels would twinkle and sparkle in the candlelight, competing to outshine one another. But their black wools, velvets, and jet adornments swallowed up all the twinkling light so that the rooms looked to have been invaded by an army of ants at best, and at worst, as if a low-lying thundercloud had entered under the sills of the sealed windows and lay low across the parquetry.

Philippe Alexandre Salvan Gondi, the Marquise du Touraine-Brissac, eldest of the Salvan sisters known collectively as the ancient aunts—and she as *Tante Philippe*—could not have wished for a better attendance. Never mind this one evening would cost her what she normally spent in a year on wax. It was worth the expense for the enjoyment of seeing her nephew Roxton's wife publicly humiliated. Which would in effect be a humiliation for him—which was her object. After all, he was the cause of the family's present fiscal misfortunes. And as her other nephew Salvan had promised to cover her debts as soon as his banishment was rescinded and he reinstated to his court position, her qualms were minimal.

Everyone and everything was in place, with the family assembled in the salon, the guests in the ballroom, and Thérése's squawking brat at the ready to be produced and laid at the feet of Mme la Duchesse d'Roxton when she gave the signal. All that was required was the arrival of her nephew's young wife, who had been led to believe she was attending a *petite soirée en famille.*

But all did not go according to plan, and from the moment Lord Vallentine strode into the salon.

In that blustering, blunt, and thoroughly uncouth way only the English were capable when expressing themselves, His Lordship dispensed with the formalities and demanded to know of his wife's family what game they were playing at. Why were they in their black when this was supposed to be a family gathering? What were they doing seated so stiffly, like a row of judges at a public execution? And what was all that noise coming from behind those doors? Was it true half the town had been invited to supper? What in the hell were the ancient aunts playin' at?

Before *Tante Philippe* had a chance to pretend ignorance and show affront, one of her sisters had a fit of hysterics. *Tante Sophie-Adelaide* had only ever experienced the affable and kind side of her niece Estée's husband. So to see Lucian Vallentine in a temper, face ripe with fury, was so startling that she fell all to pieces. Sophie-Adelaide had said from the very beginning her sister's scheming would see them all go straight to hell for their un-Christian behavior. To which Philippe retorted that as a nun that was precisely the response she expected of Sophie-Adelaide. And as a nun her sole occupation was to spend her days praying for its family members, but most of all she should pray that they had a reversal of fortune, or she would find herself without a convent cell to return to!

Seeing her twin sister in such distress was too much for *Tante*

Victoire. She blurted out to Lord Vallentine that none of this was their idea. And if the furies awaited her in Hell, so be it. But she had a more immediate and greater concern while she was on this earth, and that was to forestall the wrath of the Devil himself—their nephew Roxton.

Tante Philippe kept a brave face. Affronted by Lord Vallentine's behavior, she dared to look down her long nose at him and retort that she had not the slightest idea why or what could be so upsetting in a family gathering for supper with a few friends.

Lord Vallentine was about to tell her exactly what was upsetting when *Tante Victoire's* gangly grandson sneezed loudly. He was suffering from a head cold, but the butler mistook the nasal blast as the signal for the footmen to fling wide the double doors to the ballroom. Which they did, and with an anticipatory flourish, inadvertently revealing the extent of the family's deception.

The salon immediately flooded with light and sound from the crowded ballroom sending Lord Vallentine's blood to the boil. But before he could find words polite enough for the ears of the ancient aunts to express his fury, the guests began spilling into the salon. And they kept coming—like ants pouring forth from a disturbed nest—so that the Salvan family and Lord Vallentine soon found themselves surrounded and under siege.

The only person to keep a level head was Martin Ellicott. He had hung back by the entrance to the salon to watch events unfold from a safe distance. He had never been on this side of the great divide between master and servant before, and found it fascinating, and more exhilarating than he thought possible. When he had accompanied the Duke to various noble houses, he remained in the servant areas to await his master. Never expecting to mingle with these exalted beings, or be their guest, he could hardly believe what he was witnessing.

Here was a theatrical spectacle—the likes of which was worthy of a stage and charge for admission—so enthralling that it was some time before he realised the Duchess of Roxton was not with them. And if Lord Vallentine's blood was boiled, Martin Ellicott's turned to ice to think that he and His Lordship had failed in their one and only task—to keep the Duchess safe and in their sights at all times.

He left Lord Vallentine to deal with the societal mêlée and quickly retraced his steps, in search of the Duchess. Crossing the first salon and almost at the top of the staircase, he realised he had passed a servant girl lurking by a undraped window. He went over to her. She was moving nervously from foot to foot, hands behind her back and peering up at the ornate ceiling. She bobbed a curtsey but then let her gaze wander about the room, as if trying to appear as inconspicuous as possible. She was definitely guilty of something. Martin was about to enquire if she knew the whereabouts of Mme la Duchesse d'Roxton, when a commotion on the landing diverted them both.

The girl's mouth went slack and her eyes widened in awe at the arrival of this latest guest. But when Martin saw who it was he could not suppress his immense gratification to be finally granted every valet's wish of a lifetime—to see the labors of their sartorial hard work in action upon the societal stage. He wished George Geraghty was there to enjoy the moment with him; such was his happiness that he hugged himself and could not wipe away his grin.

Sauntering across the salon in black velvet and lace, handkerchief and gold snuffbox held aloft to showcase to maximum effect long tapered fingers and an enormous upturned cuff smothered in pieces of jet, was M'sieur le Duc d'Roxton.

His sumptuous mourning attire and expression of solemnity made him appear as if he were chief mourner at a royal funeral. And his pace was glacial, which just such an occasion would warrant, and gave his audience more time to admire him and his ensemble. It also meant that by the time he reached the second salon and framed himself in the wide doorway, the conversations, the arguments, and the general rowdiness of all those present had dropped to a murmur.

There was no need for M'sieur le Duc to be announced to a room full of his relatives and friends, but the footman did as he was instructed. It added gravitas to his arrival so that not only did all eyes turn to him, but every conversation stopped and every mouth fell open in admiration.

Seeing their nephew was such a shock to the ancient aunts that they were incapable of movement or speech. In fact, all members of the Salvan family gathered in the middle of the salon were so dazed with fright it was as if a ghost had come amongst them. *Tante Philippe* had reassured them there was nothing to worry about, that M'sieur le Duc was far away in Fontainebleau. How was it then that he was standing in the doorway, here and not there? Was he an apparition? Had he manifested in ghostly form to protect his young wife from their treachery? If anyone was capable of haunting them, it was most certainly the sinister and omniscient M'sieur le Duc d'Roxton. Such were the thoughts racing through their minds, while their startled expressions and hot faces registered their guilt.

Full of remorse and unable to contain her shame, *Tante Sophie-Adelaide* let out a muffled scream and collapsed in a dead faint. She slumped sideways off her chair, and would have slid to the floor had she not been expertly caught up in the arms of Lord Vallentine.

No one noticed. No one could take their gaze from the Duke, who now held his quizzing glass aloft to survey through one magnified eye the stunned relatives on his maternal side.

There was not a pin drop in the ensuing silence, but there was a thud when *Tante Sophie-Adelaide's* chair toppled and hit the parquetry.

SEVENTEEN

"*CHER AMI*. You did come!" exclaimed the Marquis de Chesnay, breaking from the crowd. He made his friend a magnificent bow, the lace ruffles of one wrist sweeping the parquetry, then stood to his full height in red heels and looked up at him with a welcoming smile. "I said you would. No one believed me. But here you are!"

"Your talent for the—er—prophetic never fails, Gustave," said the Duke, turning his quizzing glass on de Chesnay. "No doubt you predicted that Mme la Duchesse would be here also?"

"That too, *mon chéri*!" de Chesnay announced with a satisfied smile and look about him, before again fixing on the Duke. "I said: *Trust Gustave. They both will come! They must! Since M'sieur le Duc's marriage*—and please forgive me for my forwardness but it was said with great affection, I assure you—*Since his marriage, I said, Roxton and his divine duchess they never venture out one without the other, but always as one, like two peas in the same pod!*"

"Were you believed?

"No! Yes! Yes, that Mme la Duchesse would be here, but no, not that you would be with her. I was told you were elsewhere—"

"Elsewhere?" The Duke pulled a face and let his quizzing glass drop on its black silk ribbon to dangle between his fingers. He gently swung it back and forth. "Explain to me, if you will, Gustave, how two peas in a—er—pod can be in different places at the one time."

The silent crowd unconsciously took a step closer, eyes on the pendulum-swinging quizzing glass, ears wide open and straining to catch every word; the Duke was famed for his measured tone, and verbal eviscerations.

The Marquis de Chesnay's fat lips parted, his fingers splayed across his chest, and he glanced over his shoulder with wide expressive eyes that said *I told you so*. He could not have been more amazed had he been paid to express the gesture.

"Roxton! *Again*. That is what *I* said! I did! I *am* prophetic. But I was told most emphatically that you would not be here tonight because you had gone to Fontainebleau."

"Emphatically you say?"

"Most emphatically."

"Why would I be there when my Duchess is here? It is a mystery," the Duke said at his most congenial and baffled. He let the quizzing glass drop on its ribbon against the front of his black silk embroidered waistcoat. "But perhaps you are not only prophetic, but a solver of mysteries, too, and can provide the answer?"

"Mystery? As to that…"

The Marquis shrugged and pretended nonchalance by sticking out his bottom lip. Yet he was suddenly on the alert, head prickly hot under his wig *aile-de-pigeon*. Whenever the Duke was affable and bantered with him there was a reason behind it, and being friendly for the sake of it was not it. Everything Roxton did had a purpose. He was fishing for something, and de Chesnay was pretty sure he knew the answer, and the fish he was hoping to catch. And being a consummate courtier, he knew how to weigh up a situation and decide to whom he owed his loyalty at that moment in time. He had spent months cultivating the Marquise du Touraine-Brissac with the object of making her granddaughter his third wife. Yet his friend Roxton was a nobleman expert in the utilization of sinister methods and who had unlimited wealth to achieve his ends—not someone to trifle with, ever.

It took but a second for him to decide that perhaps it was not such a bad thing to remain wifeless for the time being; it would appease his mistress Marguerite.

"There was a time when no one here would have showed the slightest surprise to learn you had ridden post-haste to Fontainebleau to bed a delectable female," the Marquis stated with a swagger, continuing in his role of unwitting dunderhead for the benefit of their audience. "But Marguerite she was insistent: *Gustave,* she said—No! She sighed her disappointment. Truly, she did! What an angel! She sighed and said—*Gustave, sadly for those of us with aspirations of one day sharing M'sieur le Duc's couch, that time, it is no more—*" He tittered to have the Duke's unblinking gaze upon him, licked his lips and continued. "*—it is no more, because no man in their right mind, not even Roxton, would desert such a heavenly creature as Mme la Duchesse d'Roxton.*" He looked about him, nodding. "That is what she said! Truly! Every word of it. Did I not tell you—Marguerite she is an absolute angel."

The Duke inclined his head in agreement, then added, seemingly puzzled, "And yet there are those here tonight who do not share Marguerite's conviction. Therein is the greater mystery—"

"Aha! But that is easily solved because when Mme Touraine-Brissac she tells everyone you are at Fontainebleau with a certain comtesse," the Marquis interrupted without artifice and an unwavering gaze upon the Duke. "Who are we to be impolite and not believe our hostess, and in her own home. And she your aunt—"

"M'sieur le Marquis, what tales are you pouring forth into my nephew's ear?" Mme Touraine-Brissac announced without heat, sailing straight through the parting crowd like a barge on a congested river, sending her guests scurrying left and right. She tut-tutted and playfully slapped de Chesnay's arm with her closed fan. "Not fit for the ears of an elderly aunt, I'll wager. How well you look, Roxton," she continued without drawing breath, turning away from the Marquis to extend her hand to her nephew. "Marriage—or perhaps it is fatherhood, or both—has put a sparkle in your eyes; whichever it is, it suits you." And before he could respond, she turned again, and this time to address her guests, announcing with a smile, "Did I not say M'sieur le Duc he would not disappoint but attend our little soiree? And here he is! So now we shall have refreshments in the ballroom. Please! Away! Do not allow the champagne to grow tepid, and the oyster canapés to spoil! Away with you all now," she added with a smile when her guests were inclined to linger. "I need a word with my nephew alone, but be assured M'sieur le Duc and I will join you presently."

"Nicely done," the Duke complimented. "You managed to brand de Chesnay the tale bearer in this little drama of your making, while absolving yourself. He is too astute, and your guests too polite, to point the finger at the true hypocrite. That's you by the way—but allow me to settle your nerves, lest your physician be required," he added, flicking open his snuffbox and offering it to her. "Two ancient aunts collapsing on the one day is not the behavior of a good nephew, is it?"

An inveterate consumer of snuff, she eagerly took a dip into the fine powdered tobacco. And it gave her a moment to think while taking a pinch between thumb and forefinger. She placed the powder on her plump wrist. "You always have the best blend, Roxton," she confessed begrudgingly, and expertly sniffed the mixture up one nostril and then the other, and felt better for it.

The Duke offered her the crook of his arm and said conversationally,

"I have a great deal to say to you, and none of it is pleasant. But as I am a considerate nephew, I will save you the humiliation of an audience…a circumstance you were to deny my wife, I am told."

He ignored her swift upward glance as he took a moment to survey the room, where only family remained. They were milling about *Tante Sophie-Adelaide,* who was being attended to by the family physician. Lucian was one of their number, Antonia was not, but neither was Martin. So he tempered his concern and focused on dealing with the matriarch of the Salvan family.

To anyone watching, there was nothing in the Duke's demeanour, or the timbre of his voice, to suggest that just under the surface of his urbanity there bubbled an all-consuming rage he could barely contain. It had been with him since he was waylaid on the Versailles to Fontainebleau road, and made aware of the Salvan family's complicity in a plot to publicly humiliate his wife.

EIGHTEEN

Earlier, when three hours into his journey to Fontainebleau, the Duke was struck with the realisation that his chosen course of action was not only madness, it was unnecessary. All that mattered, all that he cared about, all that he loved and cherished, he had left behind in Versailles—and for what? He had never been one to allow unsubstantiated rumor to affect his actions. There were other ways and means of dealing with the Comtesse Duras-Valfons and her lurid claims. But abandoning his wife and son to do so was not one of them, and so he had turned his horse and headed for home.

As fate would have it, he stopped at an inn with his two grooms, and was taking refreshment, when a rider burst into the yard yelling for a fresh horse. The young man in dishevelled greatcoat, tricorne pulled down low on his brow, was in such a panic that everyone from innkeeper to journeyman wondered if there had been a hold up somewhere on the road, and that bandits were headed their way. But they were all reassured this was not the case. All the young man needed was a change of horse and to be on his way as quickly as possible so that he might have some hope of catching up to M'sieur le Duc d'Roxton.

At mention of such an illustrious name, there was instant activity.

Roxton's grooms gave a start to hear their master mentioned by name, because he always travelled incognito when on horseback. The Duke was not startled. He recognised the young man's voice and he rolled his eyes at Providence. He sent his men to fetch him. And when they had escorted the traveler forcibly to a corner of the yard where conversation could not be overheard, and had settled him into mute submission by threatening to knock his teeth in, the Duke joined them.

"What do you want, Montbelliard?" Roxton drawled with an uncharacteristic show of annoyance, lifting his chin out of the snug folds of his greatcoat to show his face under his tricorne.

Such was the young man's shock of relief to see the Duke, and that he had found him in time, that he lost the use of his legs. He would have crumpled but he was being propped up under the arms by the Duke's grooms, who had an even tighter hold on him now.

"Thank God! Thank God!" muttered the Chevalier, before staring into the Duke's black eyes and blurting out, "You must believe me! You will think it fantastical, but I tell you, M'sieur le Duc, that every word is the truth! I could not stand by and allow it to happen! Upon my honor, and the honor of my dearest father—God rest his soul—I tell you it is all true!"

"Before I can believe you, you need to tell me what it is I am meant to believe."

Montbelliard nodded. "Of course! Yes! My apologies, M'sieur le Duc. But where do I begin—"

"At the beginning. And do not stop until you reach the end. And you may believe me when I tell you I am all—er—ears."

NINETEEN

"MY FIRST remembrance of you was a visit to our home, and my mother sending me away with my nurse," Roxton said conversationally, strolling the perimeter of the small salon with his *Tante Philippe*, her fingers in the crook of his arm. "She pressed upon me that I must not tell my father that you had been there. But she need not have done that. I had no idea who you were. Yet, being an obedient son I never said a word.

"I was still in skirts and so naturally I was unaware of the family politics surrounding my parents' marriage: the disgrace and scandal my mother brought upon the Salvans for eloping with my father, which saw her banished from the family fold." The Duke glanced sideways at his aunt; his voice hardened. "You visited wearing your cloak of sympathetic sister. When, in truth, you were there to gather information for your brother to use against my mother—"

"What? No! That's—that's an-an *outrageous* suggestion!"

"It is fact," he interrupted flatly.

"Who said—why would they dare—"

"There is no "they". You cannot blame others. It is all there to read in the letters you exchanged with your brother. Correspondence I now own."

This revelation made Mme Touraine-Brissac look up at him, puzzled. Any concern she had that he had uncovered her deceit was tempered by her incredulity.

"Own?" She scoffed. "One does not own the personal correspondence of others. Mayhap in England—where commerce is king—it is acceptable to make such ridiculous purchases." She pouted and huffed. "Though why anyone would want such letters… But in France? No! No one in the family would dare sell, least of all purchase—"

The Duke laughed softly. "How confident is ignorance… And this from you, a skilled practitioner in the dark arts of venality! My *English* grandfather did indeed teach me that every—*thing* and every—*one* has a price. It is merely a matter of finding out what that price is. And *mon oncle* Salvan certainly had his."

"Now I know you are funning with me, Roxton!" she replied with a chuckle and unfurled her fan to flutter. "My brother would never dishonor the family name by selling off his private letters for coin!"

"How well you think you knew him. It wasn't only *his* letters," Roxton replied buoyantly. "He sold me your family's entire collection of correspondence stretching back God knows how many centuries. It now resides in my library, and is being properly catalogued by my librarian."

"I don't believe you!"

"Believe what you want," the Duke drawled. "It makes no difference to me."

"I do not understand why he would do such a thing," she muttered.

"Oh, you needn't concern yourself that he soiled the family honor publicly. He gifted the correspondence to me in his will. A discreet *gentlemanly* way of repaying a debt; I advanced him a considerable sum to settle his crippling gambling losses at Rossards."

Mme Touraine-Brissac was silent a moment. Finally she mused, "I do recall his concern about a large sum owed—I cannot remember to whom—but it was far more than he could ever repay without the family taking steps. There was talk of leaving his court duties to spend time on the family estate but—" She stopped, turned and looked up swiftly to meet the Duke's dark eyes, surprised. "—but that was some six or seven years before his death."

"Seven. I would have waited much longer. I have a—er—*talent* for infinite patience. Something else taught me by my grandfather." The corner of his mouth twitched. "A friend of my father's, Jean Chardin, said it best: *Patience is bitter, but its fruit is sweet.* I recommend highly his *Voyages en Perse et autres lieux de l'Orient.*" He glanced down. "But the travel writings of a Protestant merchant would be beneath a Salvan. And therein lies the family's weakness."

His aunt stared at him with a mixture of awe and incomprehension, quickly setting her shoulders, the family conceit firmly back in place. She mocked him. "You may have patience, and think us weak, but your arrogance could very well have been misplaced. What if my brother had reneged on your agreement? Where would your *infinite* patience have been then?"

Roxton kept his unblinking gaze on her plump face. If he was aware of the two figures in animated conversation by a window directly opposite, he did not show it, except to turn his back on them. All his concentration remained on his aunt. He grinned, as if told a good joke. But his anger was white hot.

"But he did not renege. And seven years was no time at all to wait and finally discover the depths to which you had plummeted, not only to discredit my parents' marriage but to interfere in their happiness. What you put my mother through was unconscionable, but I was prepared to leave that in the past for the sake of family harmony. And because I prefer not to dredge up painful memories. Painful for me, not you."

"How can you think I would ever—"

"You forget to whom you are speaking," the Duke cut in icily. "I am not one of your hapless relatives. I am not even of your family. I owe you nothing. In fact it is quite the opposite. Yet in deference to your son, who is not only my cousin but a good friend, and my mother's sisters, who are harmless and kind-hearted souls who only want to believe the best of everyone, I have left well enough alone—until today. I even turned a blind eye to your continued plotting with your other nephew—that creature who festers in Limoges—to have him reinstated to the court. But today your treachery crossed a line and changed —*everything*."

"Why does today hold any greater significance than any other day," she asked airily, with as much bravado as she could muster. Years spent in corridor machinations at the palace, all to further her family's—most importantly her son's—political ambitions had made her an expert in the art of emotional concealment. "You see your family and friends gathered to celebrate the return of *Sa Majesté* and the court to Versailles—oh!" She pretended a moment of clarity. "Are you disconsolate because I invited your delightfully sweet young wife without you? But I was told on the best authority—in fact by the Comtesse herself—you had gone to Fontainebleau to be with her...?"

The Duke gave an involuntary bark of harsh laughter.

"My God, if only you were a man and I could call you out! Alphonse always said you had the cullions in the family!"

"You give me more credit than is my due, Roxton," she stated, frigid at his crudity, shutting her fan with a snap. "I cannot say I've enjoyed our little stroll, but that was not your intent. Now you must excuse me. My guests await and I—"

He stepped into her path. "You will be excused when I say and not before."

She took a step back and put up her chin. "What do you intend to do to your mother's sister, and in her own home?"

"To you? Nothing. It is what I will do to ruin your eldest son's life that should concern you."

"My—my son?" Her painted face drained of color, and for the first time since entering the salon on his arm her shoulders slumped. Fear and doubt registered in her blue eyes and sounded in her voice. "Alphonse? You would ruin him? But—but he-he is your closest cousin and greatest friend! You would hurt him to get at me? Truly?"

"While I would experience true regret, because I do genuinely care for Alphonse," the Duke confessed placidly, "it would not stop me interfering in his preferred way of life. So the answer is yes, he will be made to suffer. But only if you step off the path I am about to make you walk."

"This is bluster! I am well aware of my son's unnatural inclinations," she argued, trying to disbelieve him and to regain the momentum in the conversation. "We—he and I—came to an arrangement a long time ago. He remains with his regiment, and I take care of family matters here at court, without his interference. It suits us both this way."

"I am not referring to his sexual proclivities," the Duke replied with an impatient sigh. "Whom he beds is of supreme indifference to me. Though… I fear it *would* matter to Louis. Your King is rather pedestrian in his inclinations and tastes. I doubt he would take well the news that one of his most decorated generals spends his nights tupping his golden-haired adjutant."

"It is precisely because *Sa Majesté* is prosaic that he will never believe Alphonse, Duc du Touraine's tendencies deviate from his own."

"If I tell him, he'll believe it."

"That is your threat to me?"

"No. I was merely pointing out fact. But if Louis were to find out, he would recall Alphonse from the field, and that would be the end of his military career. What a waste of a brilliant tactical mind! Louis would likely have him present himself at court, and M'sieur le Duc du Touraine as head of his family would have to obey. He loathes Versailles and all its petty intrigues. That would leave you with no role to play. But you will have each other to console—"

"Very well!" she growled and sniffed, and then lowered her voice to snarl, "What is it you want of me?"

"As mother of the Duc du Touraine, your first allegiance should be to him and his house, not to your nephew, though he be head of the House of Salvan. What you need to do is what you should have done the moment the Comte was banished from court."

"You want me to withdraw my support, and turn my back on the Comte de Salvan."

"My! You are quick on the uptake! In a word—yes. And so…?"

When she stared at him, puzzled, he lifted one brow and waited. She understood, and clearing her throat said flatly, a slight tremble in her tone,

"M'sieur le Duc has my word that I and my family will no longer offer support to the Comte de Salvan, in any capacity. The Salvan family and the House of Touraine will also cease efforts to have the Comte de Salvan rehabilitated to his inheritable court offices." She glanced up at him, adding in a rush, "Does this mean you will acknowledge Montbelliard as Salvan's heir?"

"Why would I do that?"

"Why? Why not?"

"Come now, aunt! You cannot expect me to give Salvan any glimmer of hope his title will live on after him, surely?"

"But one day Montbelliard will inherit the title; with or without your support."

"And there is your answer."

"But do you not see that if *Sa Majesté* were to officially recognise him as Salvan's heir, now, then there is every chance he would also allow him to fill the court office left vacant by Salvan's banishment. Montbelliard could then receive the inheritable pension and—"

"—you would once again be the High Priestess of Venality?"

When she regarded him hopefully, the irony lost on her, he let down his guard enough to hiss, "After what that monster did to my wife, and with your connivance, and after what you tried to perpetrate today, your expectation, as well as your judgment, is wildly misplaced."

The fierceness in his tone made her take a step away. But she was not rattled enough to enquire with a note of possibility,

"What if—what if Salvan were dead?"

"Dead? He is dead to me. Sadly, he still breathes. I am told he is in excellent health and spirits. The country air and its produce are doing him the world of good, and so he has every expectation of living another ten, twenty, thirty years or more. He will outlive you."

She moved closer so she could whisper.

"But if he were dead, you would acknowledge Montbelliard then."

"Montbelliard would inherit the title, and Louis would receive him at court. Thus your question is moot."

"But you would not stand in his way?"

"I would not."

She let out a small breath of relief, nodding.

"Madam, you have given me your word and now your family has cut all ties with your nephew in Limoges there will be no visits and no correspondence. He is a prisoner in his castle for good reason, and he is to be treated as such, by everyone. Do you understand me?"

"I do."

"And there is one other with whom you and your family will disassociate yourselves."

"Of course," she responded flatly. "The Comtesse Duras-Valfons will longer exist to us."

He extended his hand, the one with the large square-cut emerald ducal ring, not to shake hands as gentlemen are wont to do to seal a bargain, but as one does to a vassal demanding allegiance.

"Swear to it, madam."

She glanced up at him. He stared down at her, waiting. She knew what he expected of her—absolute obedience—and she knew what she must do to demonstrate this to him. She took the tips of his fingers and leaned over and kissed the ducal ring. She could barely get the words out, but she did.

"I swear upon my life and the life of my son Alphonse, Duc du Touraine, and his heirs."

"I accept your word, *tante*. But if you were ever to deviate from the path I have laid down for you, know this: Alphonse will receive by anonymous courier the packet of correspondence between you and your brother which implicates you both in the disappearance and death of one Sébastien Laval—"

"I do not know this man—"

"He was not a man," the Duke sneered. "He was a youth—they both were. He was the love of your son's life. When Alphonse refused to do his duty by the girl he had been forced to wed, you had Sébastien Laval abducted, press-ganged into the army, and put on a ship bound for the Americas, never to be seen again. The letter he left for Alphonse, the letter that broke your son's heart, was dictated under duress. You and your brother were careful to remain at arms' length. There is nothing, except your letters to one another, that can point to your involvement in Laval's disappearance. Alphonse spent years having men search for Laval at all compass points of France and beyond. I was with him when he finally received word—word that Laval had died of dysentery in the jungles of some far-flung Colonial outpost. The news broke his heart all over again. But your reaction—*Mon Dieu*, that was quite another thing altogether! It's all there in ink in your fist. You couldn't have been happier, and rejoiced at Laval's demise like a jealous lover triumphant!"

"Alphonse needed an heir. We did what was necessary for the survival of the duchy!"

"Alphonse has three brothers, and all have produced large families. Alphonse did his duty and his wife gave him four daughters in quick succession and died young. He will never remarry, and so he will never have a son, and thus no direct heir. If he were to read that correspondence, I doubt he will see your actions on his behalf as one of motherly devotion, do you?"

"Not even you would stoop so low!"

"To protect my wife and son…?" The Duke made her a magnificent bow. When he straightened there was no smile and his eyes were dead. "For them I would stoop as low as the fires of Hell."

She blinked at him, and shivered, speechless. She believed him.

TWENTY

W HEN ANTONIA entered the small attic room four of her five senses were assailed beyond what was tolerable. The room was dark and cold, it stank, and a baby was wailing. But whereas Elisabeth-Louise, Giselle, and Gabrielle fled back into the passageway, Antonia clapped a hand over her nose and mouth and resolutely sallied forth into the gloom. What she discovered so appalled her that her own discomfort and disgust were instantly forgotten, as was the fact the bawling infant was the son of her husband's ex-mistress, and could very well be his, too.

In the corner of the cramped airless space, an old woman sat hunched on a low stool, an arm at full stretch rocking a wooden crib, gaze to the floor. Bending over the crib, a reed-thin girl in threadbare petticoats was pulling faces at its tiny screaming occupant while trying to have it suck on the teat of a feeding bottle. A pile of soiled linens was heaped in a corner next to a slop bucket. There was no fireplace, and the small window was covered in so much dust there was no need for a curtain, except to help ward off the cold.

Antonia marched straight up to the crib. The old woman did

not stop her rocking, nor did the thin girl stop pulling faces. It was as if Antonia were not there at all, and she had to wonder if this was where the family locked up its idiots. She swiped the feeding bottle out of the girl's hand, took one whiff of the leaking teat and realised the girl had been attempting to quiet the infant by having it drink strong liquor. She was furious.

"*Mon Dieu, pauvre petit bébé*," she muttered, peering down at the distressed infant. "Do not cry so, *mon petit chou*," she said in the soothing voice she used with her own son. "We will soon have you warm, dry and fed. I promise you."

The infant's face was screwed up and dark red. He was swaddled, tiny body bound motionless by strips of linen cloth wound round his limbs and torso and over his head, so that he could not move at all, and all that showed were his facial features.

Swaddling done properly was not such a bad thing, and most babies were comforted by the snugness of such wrappings. Though Antonia would not have her son swaddled because her father had opposed the practice at his lying-in hospital for all but the weakest infants, saying that there was a tendency for mothers and nurses to become lazy and not change their infant out of their linens often enough.

Inspecting this infant in his wooden cradle, Antonia suspected this was one of the reasons for his distress. His linens were wet through and she would not have been surprised if he had also soiled himself several times over, such was the stench.

"Where is his wet nurse?" Antonia demanded of the old woman, then looked to the girl, who had retreated into a corner, hands up to her face. "His wet nurse? Where is she?"

"Hungry. Got no bread," the old woman mumbled. "Got no bread. Hungry."

"Get up! Show proper respect!" Gabrielle demanded, coming to stand at Antonia's back. "This is Mme la Duchesse d'Roxton, dolt!"

The old woman remained seated. But she was not deaf. She

squinted at Gabrielle, who had re-covered her mouth and nose with a handful of her petticoats, and then transferred her squint to Antonia. She looked her up and down and let out a toothless cackle, as if told a great joke. "If a fairy be a duchess, I be queen of bread!"

"We will get no sense out of her or that girl," Antonia muttered and went out into the passageway to interrogate Elisabeth-Louise and her maid.

"Are you certain the infant in that room is the child of Mme Duras-Valfons?"

"Yes, Mme la Duchesse," Elisabeth-Louise answered without hesitation.

"How are you certain?"

Mystified, the girl looked at Giselle before saying confidently, "It is the only infant in this house, Mme la Duchesse."

"That does not tell me it belongs to the Comtesse. How are you sure it is hers? Was it born in this house?"

"No, Mme la Duchesse," Elisabeth-Louise replied. "The Comtesse left it in the care of my grandmother on her way to Fontainebleau."

"That does not mean the baby in that room was birthed by her," Antonia argued. "Unwanted babies can be bought for an *écu* from any back street in Paris."

"But surely to pretend to have given birth… To then buy an infant and offer it up as your own… That is a mortal sin!" Elisabeth-Louise said, aghast.

"I do not know about that, but I do know Mme Duras-Valfons by reputation," Antonia stated. "She is not the type to worry about her sins, mortal or otherwise. If that baby is truly hers I need proof—"

"Mme la Duchesse! I know something," Giselle interrupted sheepishly, because what she knew she had discovered while eavesdropping. "I overheard the Comtesse say to Mme Touraine-Brissac that when she returned to fetch her son, the first thing she would do was check behind his left ear to make certain he was hers, and not a changeling! He has a strawberry birth mark there. I thought her jesting, but all jests have some truth to them do they not?"

"They do. *Merci*," Antonia responded. "We will look for the birthmark when he is washed and settled. But our first task is to keep him alive. He is in a very bad way in *every* way. I do not have any faith in the absent nurse. If she exists she could be another imbecile, for why did she leave him with these two? Gabrielle, send one of our footmen to fetch Cecile or Celeste, whoever is ready and willing to feed at this hour. Have her brought in my chair. It will be quicker than sending the carriage back and forth. We will find him a *nourrice* of his own tomorrow."

Gabrielle bobbed a curtsey then hesitated, saying in a whisper at Antonia's ear, "Mme la Duchesse, if he is truly the infant of the Comtesse—or even if he is not—then surely it would be for the best to leave his fate in God's hands?"

Antonia baulked.

"You think I should close the door and walk away? No! No! He is an innocent. And now we are here and I know about him I cannot allow him to suffer in the care of incompetents. You must do as I ask. Or, as I always tell you, you are free to leave me—"

"Never, Mme la Duchesse! Never. I will be with you—always."

Antonia smiled. "As I thought. Now go! We have wasted enough time! *Allez-y*! *Dépêchez-vous*!"

"How may we be of help, Mme la Duchesse?" Giselle asked eagerly.

"Find me a coverlet to wrap him in; I mean to take him to the petit apartment," Antonia said to Giselle. "And he will need fresh linens and more blankets, and an infant's shift."

When Giselle had bobbed a curtsey and scurried off down the passageway to the servants' quarters, Antonia turned to Elisabeth-Louise.

"You must find the housekeeper. The petit apartment needs a

fire in the grate. And we need a maid to bring a hip bath and warm water—"

"Perhaps he is crying because he is ill?" Elisabeth-Louise interrupted, wringing her hands, teary-eyed gaze darting over Antonia's fair hair into the room. "If we go near him, he might make us ill, too—"

"All babies cry, as you are soon to find out," Antonia replied with asperity. "And this one will stop crying when he is no longer hungry, wet, and cold. But he *will* be ill if you do not do as I ask and seek out the housekeeper—"

"I am sorry, Mme la Duchesse, but I have never been in this part of the house before. I would not know where to look, and get lost—I think too I am going to be ill!"

"Here is a coverlet, Mme la Duchesse!" Giselle announced, returning with a thin quilt, and a maid-of-all-work at her back. "This is Danielle. She is a sensible girl."

"Thank goodness for sensible girls," Antonia muttered. She smiled at the girl. "Danielle, you are to find the housekeeper," and repeated to her what she had asked of Elisabeth-Louise. When the maid-of-all-work had run off back down the passageway, she said to Giselle, "I will need your help with the baby."

"Of course, Mme la Duchesse."

"Giselle! Giselle! You cannot leave me! I am going to be ill," Elisabeth-Louise announced tearfully.

"Then you will have to be ill by yourself," Giselle retorted and followed Antonia back into the attic room.

GABRIELLE RETURNED to the petit apartment to find it full of industry, with a fire roaring in the grate, and more light. Giselle was tending to her young mistress, who was lying on the bed in the alcove with a poultice across her forehead; the Duchess was pacing the space between the door and the table and chairs, a coverlet about her shoulders for warmth; while kneeling by a hipbath were two maids with an older woman who was bathing as quickly as possible an infant whose cries of distress were affecting everyone in the room.

"It is done, Mme la Duchesse," Gabrielle announced, huffing. "The footman had no trouble borrowing a horse when the ostler saw his livery! So they should be here in time."

"I think time it is running out," Antonia reasoned sadly, regarding the infant who was now being dried. "We do not know when he was last fed. By his insistence it must have been some time ago."

"Do not worry, Mme la Duchesse. The Morvan *nourrices* will be here soon enough, and then he will stop his crying. His little lordship he is instantly at peace once he is on the breast. The silence which follows—" Gabrielle sighed and smiled. "—is a small miracle."

"*Mon Dieu*. I am the imbecile!" Antonia announced on a gasp, a thought just occurring to her. She went to the fireplace and threw off the coverlet, then proceeded to unbutton her embroidered silk jacket. "Gabrielle! Bring me a chair, then help me out of this." The jacket buttons undone, she deftly untied the bow and unlaced the front of a pair of quilted jumps. And when Gabrielle had shrugged her out of the jacket, she sat on the chair by the fire and untied the little satin bow that kept the neckline of her thin cotton chemise gathered over her breasts. Finally, she looked up. "Bring him to me."

Gabrielle hesitated, horrified. "Mme la Duchesse, we know nothing about this infant! What would M'sieur le Duc say if he knew his duchess had put to the breast an infant who is the son of —who could very well be—we know nothing about it!"

"We know that he is in misery from hunger. So it is unimportant what Monseigneur thinks," Antonia replied with a little sigh. "All I am to this infant is a means of nourishment, and M'sieur le Duc he would agree with me about that."

"And to think you had almost weaned his little lordship off your breast, too," Gabrielle said sadly.

"That, too, is unimportant to this infant."

"Yes, Mme la Duchesse."

While Gabrielle fetched the infant, it was Giselle who arranged everything for Antonia's comfort. She placed a folded blanket over the arm of the chair for padding, put another in Antonia's lap for the infant, and draped the coverlet about the Duchess's shoulders to ward off the cold.

A wailing, but scrubbed-clean baby, wrapped loosely in a white linen wrapper, was put into Antonia's arms.

"Perhaps it was fate after all that brought us here today," Antonia reasoned, gently addressing the distressed bundle in her arms. "There, there!" she soothed as the infant turned his head into the warmth of her body, instinctively searching for what he craved to end his pains, his cries punctuated with whimpers of need. "Here it is. Hush. Be still. Cry no more," she cooed, helping him latch on to suckle. "You can have all you want and more. I promise."

Everyone in the *petit apartment* except Gabrielle crept closer, fascinated, as if this was the first baby they had ever seen on the breast of a woman who was not the infant's mother. For Elisabeth-Louise this was certainly true, and she propped up on an elbow on the bed, headache forgotten as she watched in wide-eyed disbelief a duchess feed an infant from her own breast. It was a revelation.

But for the maids, for working women, infants were put out to be nursed by women who were not their mothers as a matter of course. That was nothing new in that. How else could they continue to work otherwise? What was unusual, what held them spellbound, was seeing a noblewoman giving suck; that was a once-in-a-lifetime sight. Such gently bred creatures in their silks and velvets—who inhabited a rarefied world where everyone else did everything for them—they did not nurse infants. Noble-women were too delicate, too refined, too noble, to do anything as earthy as produce milk from their breasts. Their babies were sent far into the country as soon as they were born, to be nursed and brought up by sturdy farming families, and if they survived, were returned to their parents many years later. Or so everyone in the petit apartment believed to be true, until this! It was a revelation to them too.

With the infant finally content, a peace descended on the room, which brought out an unconscious collective sigh of relief. This had Antonia looking up and about. When the women quickly looked away and went about their business, she suppressed a smile and pretended not to notice. She addressed Gabrielle.

"Please send for *café au lait*." And to Elisabeth-Louise, who had not looked away but was still staring at the infant, fascinated, she asked, "Does he have a name?"

"It is Robert, Mme la Duchesse," Giselle answered. "That is what I heard Mme Duras-Valfons call him to Mme Touraine-Brissac."

"Robert? What a fine robust name for one who has such lusty cries, *mon petit chou*," Antonia smiled, addressing the infant whose fingers were holding fast to one of hers. "And your maman she will be pleased to see that you have not been swapped for another. That birthmark is indeed the color of a strawberry. But in time, when your hair grows no one will see it." She looked up and addressed the room, saying evenly, "Now that Robert he is settled, it is time to unbolt the door on the staircase, for whoever is banging on it will surely break it down."

"Allow me, Mme la Duchesse," Martin Ellicott said evenly.

Without even a sideways glance at the Duchess, whose green eyes opened wide in surprise, he passed the startled women—all of whom had stopped what they were doing to stare at this male stranger come amongst them—and walked on through the room to the stairwell. No one said a word, though all were wondering for how long he had been there. All thought they could not be more astonished. Then out of the shadows that led to the servant passageway from whence he had appeared there stepped another. No one was left guessing as to the identity of this magnificently attired gentleman when Antonia exclaimed happily,

"M'sieur le Duc! What a delightful surprise! I am so happy you have found me!"

TWENTY-ONE

EARLIER, Martin Ellicott had been questioning Sophie, the young maid told to stand by the entrance to the stairwell that led to the entresol and say not a word as to the whereabouts of Mme la Duchesse d'Roxton. The girl obediently made no mention of the duchess, apologizing to Martin that she was unable to open the jib door because it had been bolted from the inside. It was then that Lord Vallentine strode up demanding to know the whereabouts of the Duchess.

Martin started to explain matters when Vallentine told him to leave it to him. He knew how to deal with recalcitrant menials. He'd get the girl to talk even if she didn't possess a tongue, and he'd get the door open *subito*, or he'd do the next best thing, and have it busted open. Whether he did it, or he had men have at it with pickaxes, he was getting access to whatever was behind that door!

The young maid burst into tears and crumpled to the floor. A passing footman came across to find out what was going on. Another joined him. And then an upstairs maid bustled through from the larger salon where she had been part of the contingent of servants being of assistance to the family physician. And while she tended to Sophie, the two footmen were attentively listening to Lord Vallentine's demands.

Martin tried to interrupt and tell His Lordship that there was another way, but Lord Vallentine's fury was such that he was in no mood for alternatives that did not involve breaking something. So Martin left him berating the footmen, demanding answers to questions they could not possibly answer, and went to speak with the Duke.

As it so happened Roxton had just parted ways with his ancient aunt, she returning to the larger salon while he remained on the other side of the room an interested spectator to events unfolding at the bolted jib door. He now joined Martin in the center of the room, under the chandelier.

"Allow me to guess. You've lost the Duchess," the Duke quipped.

It was said in jest but when Martin blanched, the smile died in the Duke's eyes and he pressed his lips together to await further explanation.

"Not lost, Your Grace," Martin responded awkwardly, and in English so their conversation remained private. "I think I know the whereabouts of Her Grace. But to get to that room with the least fuss—"

"—without Vallentine breaking down the door?"

"—it requires we negotiate the servant corridors."

"And you know your way about that part of this house?"

"I do, Your Grace. About many such houses."

Neither of them stated the obvious: That over the years, Ellicott had accompanied the Duke to many aristocratic houses; some were the homes of his relatives and friends, many were the residences of his various lovers. And while his master was preoccupied upstairs, Ellicott waited for him below stairs.

"Of course," the Duke replied evenly. "Lead, and I will follow."

Martin hesitated. "Should we mention to Lord Vallentine—"

"And spoil his enjoyment? I could not be so inconsiderate."

Martin suppressed a smile, turned on a heel and with the Duke left the salon to the shouts of Lord Vallentine threatening to disembowel the next fellow who dared to pretend ignorance as to the whereabouts of Mme la Duchesse D'Roxton.

SPYING A VACANT chair by the table, the Duke took it across to the fireplace where Antonia was seated, flicked out his skirts, and sat beside her. If he noticed anyone else in the cramped sparsely furnished room it was fleeting. He took a moment to find his voice—Antonia's undisguised joy at seeing him never failed to dry out his throat and cause it to constrict with emotion. Only this time he was doubly affected because she had also managed to render him speechless by her selfless act, and he was rarely moved in this way by anyone or anything.

"The delight is all mine, *mignonne*," he managed to drawl softly, clearing his throat, eyes bright, and with a smile that was for her alone. He fumbled for his quizzing-glass, and with a hand he could barely stop from shaking, lifted it to an eye he then trained on her exposed bosom. "Have you—er—run away from home to take up a vocation?"

Antonia sighed deeply and rolled her eyes. "It could not be helped, Monseigneur. I am sorry—"

"For running away? Or for taking up a vocation?"

"Silly! Neither. I have *not* run away, and after my complaints to you about *this*, do you honestly believe this is a vocation I would choose?"

He smiled and let drop the quizzing glass.

"Then you have nothing to be sorry for."

She gazed at the infant suckling contentedly, and for the first time since entering the attic and finding this baby in such horrendous conditions, emotion finally got the better of her. She teared up.

"I had to take care of him—there was no one else! If I had not…"

He pressed his clean linen handkerchief between her fingers and sat back.

"It is only natural, as a mother of an infant yourself, to want to do so."

She dried her eyes and nodded, saying on a sigh, and turning to smile at him, "All of that does not matter now you are here."

He returned her smile, and after a few moments said softly, "Thank you."

"For what, Monseigneur?"

"You humble me, and I need that sometimes."

Antonia giggled and put out a hand to him. "Renard, do not be absurd! There is nothing humble about you, and that is as it should be!"

He pulled a face, winked, and caught up her hand to hold.

When she anxiously looked toward the stairwell, distracted, he said in English, "I told Martin to wait as long as possible before drawing the bolt, short of Lucian taking an axe to the door. It will allow us a few moments for a *tête-à-tête*. Ah!" he added, reverting to the French tongue as two maids approached, "and for you to have the time to drink your *café au lait* in peace."

It was Giselle who placed the tray holding the coffee things on a small table a maid set before the ducal couple. And it was Gabrielle who prepared the coffee the way Antonia liked it and handed her the dish without its saucer. Hovering behind this activity was Elisabeth-Louise, who was determined that the Duchess not forget about her predicament; though she was sufficiently in awe of the Duke to remain mute. She approached the ducal couple with eyes downcast and bobbed a curtsey.

"Elisabeth-Louise, when next you call on the sister who lives in the villa next to ours, you are both welcome to pay me a visit,"

Antonia said kindly. "But now you must re-join your grandmother before she, too, sends a search party to find you!"

Elisabeth-Louise bobbed a curtsey. "Thank you, Mme la Duchesse. I will! I will call with Michelle. Thank you! Thank—"

"Come, Mlle," Giselle muttered, and took her charge away.

"The youngest daughter of the Duc du Touraine," Antonia informed the Duke, as he watched the girl shepherded from the room, a crease between his brows.

"That explains it. She has a great look of Alphonse—her father." The Duke settled again, adding with a crooked smile, "Does she play a part in this infant melodrama?"

"No, Monseigneur. She has a melodrama all of her own making, which I need to tell you about, but later."

"I can barely contain my excitement."

Antonia giggled again and felt better for it. "I am so happy you have come back to me!"

"I was never away from you, *ma fée*. But I apologise for my moment of madness. The ride gave me a clear head. I have decided what to do about the present—er—predicament."

"Yes, Monseigneur?"

"Nothing."

Antonia sipped at her coffee with a puzzled frown. "Nothing?"

"All that matters to me, and all that will ever matter to me, are you and Julian." Adding in English, so they could continue their conversation in private, "I have never been one to comment on spurious gossip concerning my conduct. I don't intend to start now."

Antonia's brow cleared. She was emphatic. "That pleases me. I like this idea much better."

"I'm glad you approve."

She handed off her coffee dish to Gabrielle to put the infant to her shoulder, and gently rubbed his back to induce any bubbles in his tummy to rise and be burped away. And while she did this she looked to the Duke and said in English,

"He is a well-looking baby, but you are not his sire."

The Duke's gaze flickered to the infant before he met Antonia's green eyes without so much as moving a facial muscle.

"That is a huge relief. And you know this how, *ma vie*?"

"With a father whose chief concern as a physician was the safe delivery of many babies I cannot help but know a good deal about infants, yes? I am also the proud mother of a healthy and growing four-month-old infant, who has been at my breast since his birth. And you are a most faithful and devoted husband. Oh! And I am good at arithmetic. *Et voilà*!"

The Duke inclined his head in acknowledgment of these salient points, a sideways glance at the hiccupping baby. "He does seem on the small side for one supposedly born in the Spring."

"Born in the Spring?" Antonia blew out her lips in a most unladylike manner. "He cannot be more than six or seven weeks old!"

The Duke burst out laughing at her Vallentine-esque response.

"Renard! I do not care in the least what she was like between the sheets, but the mother of this baby is a heartless witch!"

He nodded, a hand clapped to his mouth, still too overcome with laughter to speak.

Antonia glared at him, about to elaborate on her opinion of Mme Duras-Valfons as a mother, but his mirth was infectious. She grinned, suddenly realising what had made him laugh, and said cheekily, leaning into him, the infant nestled into her neck, "Now it becomes apparent to me why Julian he giggles when Vallentine makes such an absurd noise! Like father, like son!"

Their private reverie was interrupted by a loud bang above their heads. It was in fact the jib door being thrown wide, and so violently it hit the wall. There were sounds of scuffling, and shouts, and it was as if an entire battalion was rushing full-tilt down the spiral stairs. It made the Duke and Duchess sit up and take notice, while everyone in the room stopped and waited. The only sound amongst them was a querulous infant wanting its feeding to continue. All eyes peered through to the next room and at the stairwell.

Out of the gloom burst Lord Vallentine, and behind him, following at a leisurely pace was Martin Ellicott. Behind him were a number of hand-wringing footmen. His Lordship strode angrily forward, through the first room and into the second, and then he stopped and took a quick look about. He then fell back a few paces, blue eyes wide with shock.

"Roxton! You're here? Antonia! Thank God! And—" He took a step closer and squinted. "Hey! That's not my nephew!"

"Your observational skills are second to none," the Duke drawled at his most urbane.

Lord Vallentine looked over their heads at the roomful of startled maids, then back at his best friend. He was so relieved to find the Duchess safe and unharmed and with her husband that it manifested itself in the oddest of ways. He bellowed.

"What the bloody hell is goin' on here?"

TWENTY-TWO

"Tell me again the bit about Montbelliard catchin' up with you at that inn," Lord Vallentine asked as he stretched out a silver fork to the low table to pierce a slice of ham then plop it onto his plate. "That bit's still got me mystified. How did he know you'd be at that particular inn?"

"He did not," replied the Duke, handing off his tumbler to one of the footmen, careful not to disturb Antonia who was in the circle of his arm.

The family were *en déshabillé*, silk banyans thrown over their night attire and stockinged feet slipped into soft kid mules, and were enjoying a late supper by the warmth of the fire in the villa's library. Lord Vallentine and Martin Ellicott were in wing chairs opposite the Duke and Duchess who were cuddled up on the chaise longue. She had her back against his side, with her knees drawn up, and their infant son was propped on her lap amongst the folds of her embroidered chinoiserie silk banyan. She had given her infant a length of the pink satin ribbon that was still tied about the ends of her long thick plait of honey-blonde hair, and it was taking up all his concentration. Every so often she would give it a gentle tug and smile when he would squeeze his little fist tighter, determined to hold on.

"Montbelliard just happened to arrive at the inn for a change of horse," the Duke explained. "As I was about to leave it, headed for home."

His Lordship spent a few moments assembling the food on his plate into an enjoyable repast, a glance at Martin Ellicott, who was sipping his coffee in silence and watching the Duchess, and said between mouthfuls, "And he'd been prepared to ride all the way to Fontainebleau to find you? Just so he could warn you about *Tante Philippe*'s ridiculous plan to embarrass your Duchess?"

"Something like that, yes," agreed the Duke.

"I suppose Montbelliard's heroics warrant some praise on your part. But does it make you more disposed towards him and his claim to the Salvan title?"

"I will see him in private. I will do what I can for him. But I will not publicly acknowledge him or his claim while Salvan breathes."

Lord Vallentine continued to demolish a bread roll stuffed with slices of ham, cheese, and pickled onions. "Then he'll have to be satisfied with that... Damme!" he expostulated, thoughts returning to the ancient aunts. "*Tante Philippe*'s a cunning crone ain't she! But I never suspected *that* cunning. This scheme of hers was beyond the pale!"

"A scheme which you were quick to perceive, my lord," Martin Ellicott opined. "And thankfully were able to thwart in the nick of time."

"I did? I did!" Vallentine leaned in to Martin. "Tell me again how I managed to do that."

"Your initial response upon arrival at the Touraine household —one of palpable fury—was a tactical grand coup."

"Tactical grand coup?" Lord Vallentine repeated, nodding, much pleased with this description. He put up his chin. "It was wasn't it." He waved the half-eaten bread roll. "Go on if you would, and explain it to Their Graces. One doesn't like to wind one's own horn, and you were witness to this-this—*grand coup*."

"Of course, my lord," Martin replied evenly, suppressing a chortle at having caught the Duke smirking. "It was with quick-thinking precision that not five minutes—no! Not five *seconds* upon arriving upstairs to be presented, His Lordship saw what was afoot, with the family dressed formally in their mourning attire. You used the word *ambuscade,* my lord—"

"Egad! That's right! I did! Well done for rememberin', Ellicott," Vallentine replied, saying through this teeth, "That's what it was, all right. The lot of 'em lyin' in wait! Tryin' to pass off their ambuscade as a supper with a few friends! Ha! Few friends my eye!"

"And before Mme la Duchesse could respond, or, indeed, before the family could welcome us," Martin continued smoothly, "His Lordship strode in for the attack. To say he was furious, would be an understatement. Indeed, it is no small wonder Mme Sophie-Adelaide screamed and fainted. The ensuing uproar was enough of a distraction to delay and ultimately thwart Mme Touraine-Brissac's scheme."

"Couldn't have said it better if I'd said it myself, Ellicott!"

Antonia sighed deeply and turned large green eyes on His Lordship. "What a pity I was unable to witness you in action, Vallentine—"

"Yes, it was a pity, bec—"

"—because as soon as your back it was turned, I was abducted under your nose—"

"Under—under my nose?" stuttered His Lordship, rising up out of his chair, and to the bait. "Hey! Now that's unfair! I'd turned my back on you for less than that." He snapped his fingers. "How was I to know what that lot had planned—"

"Do not give yourself indigestion," Antonia complained. "I truly wish I had seen your blustering anger in action, and the reactions of the ancient aunts." She addressed Martin, saying with wide eyes and a cheeky smile of relish, "It must have been entertaining in the extreme!"

"It was that, Mme la Duchesse. And His Lordship's storming of the salon was in marked contrast to the arrival of M'sieur le Duc. Although both achieved the same ends in taking by surprise and unseating Mme Touraine-Brissac's well-laid plans."

"But of course. No one outshines M'sieur le Duc in any salon. He is always *magnifique*," Antonia stated proudly. She tilted her face up to her husband. "I wish I had seen you make your *grande entrée* under the chandelier! Even in the gloomy entresol, you were a sight to behold in your black velvet and jet." She smiled cheekily, adding softly, "But I much prefer you undr—"

Roxton stopped her with a gentle kiss, and murmured, barely able to keep a straight face, "Behave."

She pouted, pretending disconsolance, but she also could not hide the laughter in her eyes. "But I do not intend to *behave* at all later, when we—"

He kissed her again, but this time it was their son's loud squealing which left her sentence hanging and ended the intimate moment between the couple. Their infant was flapping his arms, and he had clutched in his left fist the pink satin ribbon, tugged free from his mother's hair.

"*Quel singe effronté!*" Antonia exclaimed, chuckling. She leaned forward and kissed her son's rosy cheek, nuzzled him, then kissed his fist, while deftly removing the long length of satin ribbon from between his fingers so she could secure her plait before it unravelled. "Are you wanting to steal Dennis's thunder from your papa, JuJu! *Hein?*"

"Plenty of time before he does that!" Lord Vallentine exclaimed gruffly, making motions to take his leave. He set aside his plate and pulled his banyan closer about his chest, then stood and said, expelling a breath, "It's been a long day for all of us, and I've got an early start. Meetin' Montbelliard at *la Grande Écurie*—"

"You are embarrassed that I shared a kiss with Monseigneur?"

Antonia stated curiously. "I apologise for your embarrassment, but I do not apologise for the kiss. And I do not want you to leave yet. I must thank you for—"

"No need for that!"

"Antonia asked you to stay, Lucian," drawled the Duke, and with his eyes told him to sit.

Vallentine sat, but on the very edge of the wingchair's cushion and with his hands between his knees, like a naughty schoolboy, which only highlighted his discomfort and proved Antonia's point. So did the fact he was forced to wait while she said her goodnights to her infant before handing him off to his nurses. He watched the women bustle away with their ducal charge, so wrapped in thought about his impending fatherhood that he nodded when addressed by Martin Ellicott, but with no idea what he had said. That is until a footman stood before him with a tray that had upon it a crystal carafe and tumblers. He mechanically took the tumbler of brandy, and it almost slipped through his fingers with Antonia's next words.

"I love you, Lucian," Antonia said gently, and smiled when he blushed scarlet. "You are the best of brothers. What you did today at *Tante Philippe's* soiree, to want to protect me and to defend M'sieur le Duc's honor, was heroic. We truly believe that, do we not, Renard?"

"We do."

"So you must never think we do not appreciate you. But me," she added, dimpling. "I like to tease you! And who else can I tease if not *mon beau-frère?*"

"And after your part in today's little—er—drama, I do not doubt you still have questions," said the Duke, and sipped at his brandy. He smiled crookedly. "And I would prefer to provide the answers than you rely on what your wife tells you in her letters."

Vallentine did not sip. He threw back the brandy in one gulp and stuck out his tumbler to have it refilled. With the replenished tumbler settled on his silken knee, and a sidelong glance at Martin

Ellicott who was also nursing a brandy, he cleared his throat and said,

"I do. But you might prefer not to answer 'em. And that is your right and—"

"It is," interrupted the Duke. "But, believe me, you have earned your answers, Lucian. And I keep few secrets from those present." He huffed. "And those remaining few I do have I do not doubt Martin knows and has the answers. So there we are—ask away!"

TWENTY-THREE

"IN THAT CASE, I have two questions that still have me baffled since I barged down that stairwell and found you both." His Lordship leaned forward, tumbler now in his hands and asked quietly, as if he feared being overheard, "There ain't any way of puttin' this delicately, so I'll just come out and ask it: That infant Mme la Duchesse was-was—nursing. Who does he belong to, eh?"

"He is the son of the Comtesse Duras-Valfons and her husband the Baron Thesiger."

Vallentine raised his tumbler and snorted. "Aye! If that's what you want everyone to believe, then that's what I'll say."

Antonia cocked her head, confounded. "You do not believe Monseigneur?"

"I'll believe whatever he tells me to believe, but between us, if that infant was sired by Ravenous Ricky, I'll swallow my own shoe!"

Antonia sat up tall. "I do not care in the least what the ancient aunts have been told, or what Madame said to you in her letters, or what the general gossip is, but that infant was not sired by M'sieur le Duc—"

"No! No! That wasn't what I was implyin'! On my honor! Have you ever met Thesiger?"

"No. That pleasure awaits me."

His Lordship gave another snort. "Pleasure? Ricky is more a fair-day attraction! He has been since he was at Eton with us. He's a glutton par excellence. Why do you think he's called Ravenous Ricky, eh? I doubt he's seen his toes these past ten years or more."

The Duke swirled his brandy and looked across at his best friend. "All that matters is that he is married to the Comtesse Duras-Valfons. And any offspring is theirs, regardless of whether his alarming—er—circumference is an obstruction to performing his conjugal duties, or not."

Lord Vallentine pulled a face of disgust, then glared at the Duke, a significant sidelong glance of warning at the Duchess. But her response was so refreshingly straightforward he had to wonder why he was worried at saving her blushes.

Antonia touched the Duke's hand. "To have such a husband must make the Comtesse feel keenly the loss of you as a lover. So I am a little sorry for her. But only a little. I would feel more, but I cannot after her neglect of her infant." She had a sudden thought. "Monseigneur! Regardless of whether her ravenous husband is capable of performing his husbandly duties or not, any infant she has is considered her husband's under the law, *n'est-ce pas?*"

"Yes," agreed the Duke and kissed the back of her hand. "Which is why I stated that he is the son of the Comtesse Duras-Valfons and her husband the Baron Thesiger."

Antonia's eyes narrowed. "Then I take back my sympathy! To call into question her son's parentage is a thing most monstrous! I do not care how *grossièrement gras* he is, if he is the father of that infant or not, her son deserves an inheritance. And so, if Baron Thesiger owns him, then he is his son. *Voilà!*"

"Regardless of her abhorrent behavior towards us, be assured Baron Thesiger will not be deprived of the opportunity of having an heir."

"You mean to tell him?" asked Lord Vallentine.

"I do. As I recall from our Eton days, Ravenous—er—Ricky was not an unpleasant fellow. Dull. But there was no spite in him. A letter will be dispatched on the morrow, alerting Thesiger that his wife abandoned her infant for the pleasures to be had at Fontainebleau, leaving him in the care of an old crone, an idiot girl, and a negligent wetnurse." The Duke sipped his brandy. "The infant could not possibly do worse if Thesiger decides to own him."

Antonia was anxious. "Will he take him, Monseigneur?"

"It is possibly his only opportunity of having a legal heir." Adding gently to quell her anxiety, "Thesiger is not an unkind man, *mignonne*. In fact, I believe he will be grateful and do right by him."

"Then it pleases me very much he is to be the infant's papa," Antonia replied. "And I will tell you what else pleases me…" She looked across at Martin with a smile, but addressed His Lordship, "Knowing what Lucian will be having for his breakfast!"

"Eh? Breakfast? Why does what I eat for breakfast please you?"

If His Lordship was mystified, Martin Ellicott was not, and his shoulders were already shaking with laughter.

"Mme la Duchesse," he asked, chuckling. "What do you suggest—a sauce Isigny or a bechamel as an accompaniment to shoe leather?"

Everyone laughed except Vallentine.

"Oh! Ha ha! Have your joke! But I'm not the only one who'll be eatin' shoe leather for breakfast when they hear Ravenous Ricky Thesiger has an heir! Besides which, that she-devil his wife is sayin' otherwise, so I don't know how you're goin' to manage puttin' that gossip to rest."

"What others think is unimportant," Antonia said dismissively. "All that matters is what Monseigneur's family—" She stared at one and then the other. "—*you*—think."

Martin Ellicott and His Lordship looked at one another, clinked tumblers, then raised them to their hosts. "Hear! Hear!"

"I'll tell you somethin' for nought," opined Lord Vallentine. "I'm no expert on infants, but Thesiger's brat looked a bit on the small side if he's supposed to have been born around the same time as my nephew."

"Estée did give you the entire sordid story doing the rounds, didn't she!" quipped the Duke.

Lord Vallentine squirmed on his chair and wracked his brain for a suitable response that would not implicate his wife nor offend his best friend. Antonia came to his rescue, and he audibly sighed his relief.

"When your own infant arrives, you will get to know him intimately and see how quickly he grows. And so these things will no longer be a mystery to you," she lectured. "But I commend you in seeing a difference in the two infants because most people would not! All they see are two babies. When to anyone who has spent time around babies would know that a baby at six weeks old is vastly different in size and abilities to one who is four months old." She shrugged and stuck out her lip. "Those at court have not a clue about their babies because as soon as they are born they send them away! Which is inconceivable to me, and very sad. I could no more send Julian away as stop breathing!"

"Why do they send them away?" Vallentine asked conversationally. "After all the time and trouble of being enceinte, not to mention the birth, and then to send them off like that? I'm fairly mystified m'self!"

As soon as he asked this he suddenly sat up and blinked, greatly surprised to discover he was genuinely interested in the answer and the topic of babies in general. He happened to glance across at the Duke and found him watching him with a knowing smile and a lift of his brow. And then he knew, at that moment, that his revelation was no longer private, and he was not the only one to have experienced it. He grinned bashfully and gulped down the last drops of brandy.

"They are sent to the country to be brought up by others," Antonia told him. "And there they stay until they are no longer infants! Some parents venture to visit once in a while to assure themselves their child still lives and is thriving, but most do not."

"That didn't happen to you, or to the Duke and his sister."

"My separation came at a later date," the Duke stated flatly, sighed, and rallied himself to add, "But no, my parents did not send us away. They were however considered peculiar in the extreme to want to keep their children underfoot. No doubt as we are continuing the family tradition, we will also be thought peculiar—"

"But we do not care about that in the least, do we, Renard?"

"We do not."

Lord Vallentine looked to Martin. "What about you, Ellicott? Were you sent away to the country as an infant?"

"My parents were already in the country, my lord. And no, they did not send me away. Even when the fourth duke offered to pay the expense of sending me to a local boarding school."

"Dear me, Martin! To have extracted a pecuniary sum from the fourth duke, you must indeed have been troublesomely underfoot! Good for you!"

"Thank you, Your Grace."

"And you, Lucian," Antonia asked. "Were you sent to the country as an infant?"

"I think it might be different for infants in England. But I don't have a recollection of life before about the age of Eton, I'm afraid," Vallentine apologized.

Antonia pulled a face. "Eton is not an age. It is a village and a school."

"Ha! That's what you think! For me, there's *Before Eton*, and then there's *Eton*, and then there's *After Eton*. Before Eton, well those bits are fuzzy. I was shuffled off to boarding school almost as soon as I went from skirts to breeches. I'd say I was about six years old—"

Antonia was horrified. "Six? *Mon Dieu*! That is diabolical!"

Lord Vallentine shrugged. "Possibly. But I knew no different. And a few years later Roxton turned up to keep me company, and then life truly began!" He frowned. "You hated me at first. Threw rocks at me, and mud."

"Don't take it to heart. I hated everyone."

"Aha! So you did. And obviously I didn't because here I still am!" He had a sudden thought and asked Antonia, "These infants that are farmed out… If their parents don't see 'em from one year to the next—how do they know when they next see their infant grown it's the same one as the one they handed over?"

Antonia shrugged. "That is a very good question, Lucian. I cannot answer you."

Lord Vallentine was aghast, and he shot out of his chair. "That settles it! My son ain't bein' farmed out anywhere. He's stayin' right here. I don't care what Estée says. She can throw as many tantrums as she can marshal, but I won't flinch!"

"You may rest easy, Lucian," the Duke said placidly. "My nephew will be raised underfoot with his cousin, whether you and my sister care for it or not."

"Good! You can tell her so."

The Duke smiled crookedly. "Yes, I thought that task might fall to me."

"Do not worry, either of you," Antonia stated. "Madame will not want her infant sent away. She does not wish to nurse him, but she will coddle him."

"May I know, my lord, what made up your mind?" Martin Ellicott asked.

"Ain't it obvious? If I farm him out, how do I know I'll get the same one back? No! He'll be under my nose day and night until I can be sure I know just by lookin' at him he's mine!"

"That takes care of the first two days of his life," the Duke murmured. He asked audibly, "You had another question?"

Lord Vallentine snatched up a tapestry cloak bag that was beside his chair and unceremoniously dumped its contents on the low table, creating a heaped pile of fabric swatches, paper notes, lengths of cord and ribbon, squares painted various shades of reds, blues and yellows, and swatches of patterned paper. Antonia and Martin leaned forward in wonderment at the array of samples for what appeared to be wallpaper, paint, and upholstery. The Duke knew at once what they were for and who they were from, and chuckled to himself.

"This lot arrived from the lady wife while we were with the ancient aunts," Lord Vallentine explained, staring down at the pile and scratching his head through the soft silk of his tasselled night-cap. "Accordin' to her letter, I have some tough choices to make for the redecoration of my bedchamber, closet, and Pearson's room…" He suddenly frowned across at the Duke. "Was this your idea?"

"It was. And a well-timed one."

"She'll be here at the end of the week, and she'll have a couple of *marchands-merciers* in tow. Because it seems we can't just have new paint and carpet, furniture and curtains, but need a whole host of *objets d'art* to go with it! And I'm expected to choose, and *she's* expectin' a result!"

"Madame's morning sickness has disappeared?" Antonia asked, surprised.

"Mornin' sickness?" Lord Vallentine repeated. "Come to think on it… She never mentioned it in her letter."

"With an entire apartment to redecorate and refurnish, and cram to the ceilings with *objets d'art*, why would she?" the Duke drawled.

Antonia's eyes went wide, she turned and fell against the Duke, and tilted her face up to him. "Oh! Renard! You are so very clever!"

Roxton winked and brushed the tip of his nose against hers with a roguish grin. "I am, am I not?"

"Hey! Hey! Attend to what's important here!" Lord Vallentine complained.

"Which is what, my lord?" Martin asked.

All three looked at His Lordship expectantly.

He regarded his family in panic. "What, in the name of all that's holy, am I supposed to do with this lot?"

TWENTY-FOUR

Elisabeth-Louise's sister and the Roxtons' neighbor, Michelle Haudry, was shown into the library by the butler. He escorted her halfway up the long room, and then left without a word. She was too polite to look about, and stared straight ahead at the nobleman seated behind a large desk piled with parchments and books. He did not look up and continued writing as if she were not there at all. Her gaze shifted to the servant standing silently by his master's chair holding a pounce pot. But as he did not acknowledge her either, she wondered if perhaps the timing of her visit was inopportune. But as she had not been turned away at the door, she could only assume that her presence was not entirely unwelcome.

It did not take a giant intellect for her to immediately realise it was the master of the house busy with his quill. She'd had glimpses of M'sieur le Duc d'Roxton from her upstairs window, while he was in his garden strolling with his duchess in the winter sunshine. But now, being just feet away from him, she could see that he was exceedingly handsome, made all the more so by his attire, dressed as he was in black velvet and white lace, a chinoiserie silk banyan about his shoulders, and his natural black hair tied at the nape with a large white silk bow.

She was not a timid person, and as the daughter of a duke she was not in awe of his nobility. But there was something about M'sieur le Duc d'Roxton that was compelling—an aura—Yes! That was what it was! It was an aura of sinister authority and restrained decadence which she found fascinating, but it also caused her to give a little shiver.

Her first instinct was to bob a curtsey, apologise, and retreat. Then she remembered her duty as a wife, a sister, and as a daughter. And that she was here, not on a social call, but to achieve an outcome satisfactory to all parties, one that would ensure, not only her sister's future, but the future of the family into which she had married.

Squaring her shoulders, she was resolved to approach the desk when a sweet voice interrupted her thoughts and glued her mules to the floor.

"Mme Haudry! How lovely of you to pay us a visit. Please excuse me for seeing you here in our library, but my brother-in-law has turned my morning room into a showroom for the creative genius of M'sieur Meissonier! Won't you please join me for *café au lait?*"

Michelle Haudry spun about and there standing before an upholstered sofa, book in hand, was a diminutive beauty in a robe volante of lemon-yellow lampas woven with silver threads and green silk. Again recognition came from her glimpses of the Duchess in her garden. Again, she was surprised. First by the Duke, and now by his duchess, who was not only arrestingly beautiful with the most mesmerizingly green eyes, but ever so tiny. Elisabeth-Louise said the Duchess was not unlike a fairy come amongst them; for once Michelle did not think her sister exaggerating.

"Mme la Duchesse! My-my apologies," she replied with a

blush, because she realised she had been staring. She sank into a deep curtsey. "I did not see you there."

"Perhaps I need three inches on my heels and not two, *hein*?" Antonia replied with a smile and indicated the sofa opposite and resumed her seat. She set her book beside a pile of opened letters, and put her hands in her lap; Michelle Haudry noticing that the Duchess's wrists were covered with pearl bracelets, one set with a painted cameo of the Duke. "I am happy to finally make the acquaintance of our neighbor. Although I cannot say it is serendipitous because I am told our maids contrived the outcome. Is it not a small world? But one I am glad of, for it has allowed us all to live to suit everyone."

Before Michelle Haudry could respond, the Duchess gave a signal to the two attending footmen by the morning tea trolley to place the silver tray holding the coffee things and a plate of macarons on the low table between them.

"And it is my turn to apologize. Please excuse our state of undress," Antonia continued conversationally. "I told M'sieur le Duc to expect a visit from you later in the day, but not this soon after breakfast. So you will have to take us as you find us. Perhaps there was some misunderstanding on my part as to the timing of your visit?"

If the couple in their sumptuous fabrics were in undress, it was another surprise for Michelle Haudry. But she did her best to rein in her astonishment and said as evenly as she could manage, "No misunderstanding by you, Mme la Duchesse. It is my fault entirely. I have interrupted your morning, but I needed to speak with you without my sister present."

"Oh? Does she know, or perhaps you will both be returning this afternoon?"

"That will all depend on the outcome of this visit," Michelle Haudry replied distractedly, watching the footmen pour out coffee into two of three dishes. "She—Elisabeth-Louise does not know I am here."

"Then let us hope the outcome is what you want," Antonia replied with a smile, and handed her guest one of the filled porcelain dishes then sat back to sip her coffee. She made no further comment but it was obvious from her expression that she expected her guest to provide her with further explanation for her intrusion into their morning solitude.

"Mme la Duchesse, Elisabeth-Louise visited me yesterday evening and told me of the extraordinary events which unfolded at the house of our grandmother. To say I was astonished is an understatement. But after speaking with her maid, I was reassured that what I was told was indeed a true account. Though I confess I am still in awe of your selflessness with an infant unknown to you who—"

"Please, Mme Haudry. You are a mother. I did what any mother would do for a distressed infant."

"No, Mme la Duchesse," Michelle Haudry contradicted flatly, setting aside the milk jug and taking up her coffee dish. "No mother of my social circle would have had your presence of mind. I include myself in that assessment. I have three daughters, two are still in leading strings, but I've had nurses to feed and water them since birth." She sipped at her coffee, and then looked into the Duchess's eyes and said evenly, "Mme la Duchesse, I know you are aware of Elisabeth-Louise's—*predicament*, and that she has petitioned you to help her. I decry her impetuousness, and apologise on her behalf. She should not have put you in the position of confidante. That has led to an obligation on your part, of which I am certain she is very aware. Elisabeth-Louise has always been one to take the shortest path to get what she wants, without a care to the risks. And what she wants is to be the wife of the Chevalier Montbelliard, and so she has done all in her power to force my father's hand to agree to the match."

"You somehow blame yourself for your sister's predicament?" Antonia asked curiously. "You should not. When the heart rules the head, and one is in the moment, the consequences they are unimportant. You flinch at that simple truth, but I tell you that it is only natural for two people in love to give in to their feelings. *Et voilà*! And now there is her predicament." Sensing a presence, she looked up. "Am I too blunt, Monseigneur?"

"Not at all," drawled the Duke, joining them. "Not blunt but candid. And ever truthful. Forgive my preoccupation in not welcoming you when you first arrived, Mme Haudry. That was the last of my correspondence for today."

"That pleases me," Antonia said happily, and bunched up her petticoats so he could sit beside her. "Now you can drink coffee with us."

Michelle Haudry was up off the sofa and down into a curtsey in one fluid movement. And when the Duke made her a bow of recognition, not only of her presence but of her station as the daughter of the Duke du Touraine, she swallowed a lump in her throat, too overcome to speak.

The Duke pulled the silk banyan closer across the front of his black velvet waistcoat and sat beside his Duchess. If either realised their guest was emotionally fraught, they pretended not to notice, and it was left to the Duke to bring Michelle Haudry out of her abstraction with a blunt assessment of his own.

"You do not look at all like your father, Mme Haudry."

Michelle Haudry resumed her seat, more at ease and said with a huff of laughter, "That is true, M'sieur le Duc. Elisabeth-Louise greatly resembles *notre père*. I inherited his brains, she his beauty."

Roxton said to Antonia, "You see. Mme Haudry and I were both being candid. Though she is too harsh on herself."

"Mme la Duchesse, if M'sieur le Duc had been blunt he would have said I was the plain sister in my family."

"M'sieur le Duc is always truthful. You *are* too harsh," Antonia stated. "You have a lovely countenance, and dark expressive eyes. And those who are blessed with great beauty but no brain quickly grow tiresome; they then dull not only the eyesight but also desire. M'sieur le Duc will tell you so himself."

"I would, but you just did, *mignonne*," quipped the Duke. He regarded Mme Haudry over the gold rim of his coffee dish. "Shall we get down to business? As you have come alone, and at this hour, I presume you have been sent as emissary, so that should the outcome of this meeting prove disappointing to you, you can then beat a retreat with your father's honor—and your father-in-law's considerable fortune—intact."

This was news to Antonia. She latched on to the one word that did make sense to her. "Sent? *Pourquoi donc?*"

"M'sieur le Duc is correct, Mme la Duchesse," Michelle Haudry explained evenly. "I was sent. Not by my father, but by my father-in-law André Grimold Haudry. We—my father-in-law and I—thought it best to keep my father in ignorance until after this meeting."

"The Duc du Touraine is unaware his youngest daughter has been—er—impregnated by the Chevalier?"

Michelle Haudry blushed scarlet but her tone remained even. "That is so, M'sieur le Duc."

"And what of the Chevalier's proposal of marriage?"

"The Chevalier has written again to my father, but has yet to receive a reply. And that is because my father is awaiting my response."

"Your father puts a high value on your opinion."

"He does, M'sieur le Duc."

Antonia looked from the Duke to Mme Haudry, and back to the Duke, and asked anxiously, "I do not understand. Surely Elisabeth-Louise's papa would welcome a match between the Chevalier and his daughter? Montbelliard is presently poor, but as heir to the Comte de Salvan there are any number of creditors who would willingly lend him funds. And the Duc du Touraine he does not need to know the other news until after they are married. And so that dilemma it solves itself, *hein?*"

The Duke held her hand on his velvet knee and said gently, "Were it that simple, *ma vie*."

"Why—why is it not, Monseigneur?"

Before the Duke could respond, Michelle Haudry jumped into the brief silence with further explanation.

"I have been given permission by my father-in-law to make you an offer, M'sieur le Duc. If the terms are acceptable, then I do not doubt my father will be favorable to the match, particularly when he learns of my father-in-law's generosity, but most particularly when he is assured you are not against the union." She smiled thinly. "He never held out much hope of Elisabeth-Louise making a splendid match, given her impetuous temperament. So he will be overjoyed. The marriage will of course then proceed with all speed, given my sister's—um—*predicament*." She addressed Antonia with a soft smile, "It will please everyone, and only a few of us will be unsurprised, that not long after the wedding, the couple announce they are expecting. So, yes, *that* dilemma it will solve itself, Mme la Duchesse."

Antonia returned her smile, but she was still anxious. "You say *that* dilemma, so I must presume there are other dilemmas of which you are both aware, but I am not."

"That is true, Mme la Duchesse," Michelle Haudry stated, a glance at the Duke who sipped his coffee in silence. "And only M'sieur le Duc and my father-in-law are capable of resolving those."

"I perfectly understand why the Chevalier must marry your sister at once," Antonia replied. "And I understand why you do not wish to upset your father with your sister's predicament, for surely it would only make him ill-disposed toward the Chevalier. What I do not understand, is the interest of your father-in-law, and why it is necessary for you to be his emissary. Nor do I understand why M'sieur Haudry is making you an offer, Monseigneur," she added, gaze turning to the Duke, "for surely this is for the Touraine family to resolve? Yet even the Duc du Touraine wants your approval? So it is you who hold the key. But to what?" She threw up a hand. "*Je suis perdue!*"

"Most everyone would be just as lost as you, *ma vie*," the Duke replied with an understanding smile. "I will try to explain matters in the simplest of terms. Not because I think you incapable of understanding it any other way, but because I believe Mme Haudry's father-in-law is at this very minute at her house pacing the carpet, awaiting her return with my response—?" When Michelle Haudry nodded, he continued, "And because there is every possibility Vallentine will interrupt us with some banal question of earth-shattering importance to him about which wallpaper better matches the cloth for the curtains to his closet."

TWENTY-FIVE

T HE DUKE explained the situation this way:

"First, it is necessary for me to describe the important position held by Mme Haudry's father-in-law. He is one of the forty of France's *fermiers généraux*. These men control a vast network that collects the taxes and duties owed to the Crown by its subjects; taxes that are placed on everything from salt to tobacco. It is a vastly complicated business involving hundreds of people employed in various roles, from administrators to what amounts to personal troops to enforce payment of bad debts. And for administering and collecting these taxes on behalf of their King, each Farmer-General receives a substantial bonus from the royal treasury.

"This system of taxation has made these men exceedingly wealthy, which means not only do the populace think them greedy and hate them, so do the nobles because the *fermiers généraux* are wealthier than they, own houses and estates they envy, and because they are not required to spend their days playing at courtiers here at the palace; their lives are unfettered by royal duty. You may correct me, Mme Haudry, but I believe your father-in-law André Grimod Haudry is one of the wealthiest of the *fermiers généraux*."

"He is, M'sieur le Duc."

"And my précis for the Duchess on the nature of M'sieur Haudry's business? You concur?"

"Yes, M'sieur le Duc," Michelle Haudry replied, though she could not help a wry smile when she continued, "What I would add for Mme la Duchesse's benefit is that while the *fermiers généraux* as a collective are hated by the populace and envied by the nobility, there are individual Farmers-General who use their wealth as patrons of worthwhile projects and the promotion of exceptional artisans, and in doing good works for the church. My father-in-law is one such, and perhaps he is a little less hated than most."

The Duke inclined his head in acknowledgment of her opinion.

Antonia toyed in thought with the pearl bracelets on her wrist, hand still in her husband's warm clasp, and said with a frown, "Monseigneur, while I have a better understanding of M'sieur Haudry's position as a *fermier général*, I am still lost. I am sorry, but I still do not understand what any of this has to do with Elisabeth-Louise's marriage to the Chevalier Montbelliard. Or the Duc du Touraine's reliance on your good opinion before he will give his consent."

"There is no need to apologise, *mignonne*, because I have yet to explain those connections." He handed off his dish on its saucer to a hovering footman. "Shall I continue?"

Antonia nodded and resettled on the sofa, both hands now in her lap, and back straight. She smiled at the Duke and said brightly, "I am confident that once you explain *everything* I will understand. So please continue." She had a sudden thought. "Oh! Unless, of course, Mme Haudry, you wish for another dish of coffee…?"

Michelle Haudry shook her head, quick to suppress a smile at Antonia's enthusiasm. "No, Mme la Duchesse. I am quite replete."

"And you will I hope excuse the need for M'sieur le Duc to offer me further explanation. While I find it fascinating to learn new things, you who know it all already, may be bored. But I assure you that M'sieur le Duc he is an excellent *précepteur*, and so perhaps you will learn something too, yes?"

"Thank you, *ma vie*, but I can assure Mme Haudry that I will be to the point—"

"Oh yes!" Antonia interrupted, adding with relish, "Because her father-in-law he is at this very moment wearing her carpet to threads! I will not interrupt again."

"That would be for the best in the circumstances. Remember Vallentine and his wallpaper samples."

"I have not forgotten! He will be here soon enough, as I promised to offer my opinion on his choice of colors. So when he interrupts you must remember that it is not entirely his fault—oh! Forgive me. I will be quiet now and listen." She lifted her chin and cocked her head. "You have all my attention. *S'il vous plaît, continuez!*"

"Thank you, *mignonne*," the Duke said gravely, though there was no disguising the laughter about his eyes.

Overcome by a sense of joy at the playful interaction between the ducal couple, Michelle Haudry was forced to stifle a giggle. With his wife, this austere nobleman transformed into an entirely different being from the one of common report. She felt privileged to be in their company, and she certainly had learned something new. It was such a rare moment she wished she could hold on to it for herself, but of course she would share it with her father-in-law who would appreciate this rare insight into this most enigmatic duke. However, it did not stop her being mortified to have giggled in their presence; if the Duke and Duchess heard, they chose to ignore it and the Duke carried on.

"Regardless of M'sieur Haudry's enormous wealth and position within the tax-collecting fraternity," the Duke was telling Antonia. "Or his stature in Parisian society amongst the bourgeoisie, his influence does not extend to the palace and the court of his king. And without influence at court, M'sieur Haudry has little chance of obtaining what he most desires in this world."

"But surely with his wealth, he can have anything he wants?"

"He can, and he does. But there is one thing no amount of coin can buy."

Antonia was mystified and remained mute, awaiting enlightenment. The Duke leaned in and said quietly, "He craves the ear of his king."

This surprised her. "As a wealthy bourgeois can he not approach *Sa Majesté's* ear?"

"He can. But that ear is deaf to him, you see, because he does not have the requisite nobility to be heard."

Antonia thought about this a moment. "But… If M'sieur Haudry's daughter-in-law is the daughter of the Duc du Touraine, then surely that connection brings him a step closer to the King's ear?"

"It does. But as M'sieur le Duc du Touraine prefers to keep his distance by remaining with his regiment, he is too many steps away from his king to be heard. And so this does M'sieur Haudry no favors."

"France's most decorated general does not wish to exert himself on behalf of his daughter's father-in-law?"

If the Duke was surprised Antonia chose to speak in English, he did not show it. Although he understood why—so that their guest remained in ignorance of their conversation—so he answered her in kind.

"That is an astute observation, my love. You are correct. The Duke prefers to keep his—er—fingers far from the political flame. He leaves court intrigue to his mother—"

"Aunt Philippe?"

"Yes. She is far more adept at currying for favor. Or I should say she *was*, but as a Salvan—"

"—she lost what influence she had at court when the Comte de Salvan was banished," Antonia stated, finishing off his sentence with a nod of understanding. "That is too bad for the father-in-law of our guest. No doubt he thought with his son's marriage to the daughter of a duke, he would gain access to the King's ear. When in fact he has found himself aligned to a family that is in disgrace."

The Duke smiled at her grasp of the political corollaries. "*Touché*, my darling."

Antonia glanced at Mme Haudry who remained impassive. Reverting to her native tongue, she said to the Duke with a knowing smile, "But as you have the ear of *Sa Majesté*, it seems M'sieur Haudry now wishes you to whisper in that ear for him."

"That would be my best guess. Yes."

"I wonder what he wishes you to say?"

"Perhaps we should ask Mme Haudry?"

The Duke and Duchess both turned and regarded Michelle Haudry at the same moment. If their guest was at all intimidated, she did not show it. In fact, she surprised them with an admission neither saw coming.

"I beg your pardon, but I should reveal, lest you think me eavesdropping, that I not only understand the English tongue, but I read and write in that language too. I am also proficient in Italian and Spanish." Her smile was unnecessarily self-deprecating. "My father-in-law says my linguistic skills are a great asset to his business and go some way in compensating for the Salvan family's disgrace."

The Duke inclined his head. "Thank you for your honesty, Mme Haudry. I do not doubt that your intelligence is better appreciated by your husband and father-in-law than it ever was by your own family."

"M'sieur le Duc is sincere, Mme Haudry," Antonia assured her. "Monseigneur he tells me that the girls of the bourgeoisie are better educated than most daughters of the nobility, which makes them worthier companions and more valued by their husbands. You and I, we are the exception for our class, yes, because we too are educated. So I do not doubt the family you married into value your accomplishments. Is that not so, Monseigneur?"

"It is, and I do believe Mme Haudry has my measure," quipped the Duke. "And yours, *mignonne*. As we have hers." He held Michelle Haudry's gaze. "You find my ears wide open, madam."

The Duke and Duchess awaited her response.

"My father-in-law does indeed wish M'sieur le Duc to whisper near the ear of his king," she admitted. "But he does not want you to do anything so gauche as to whisper directly into it. What he wants is to be brought to the notice of the King's mistress Mme de Pompadour, and if a meeting might be arranged with her."

"For the purposes of what?"

"In the first instance?" Michelle Haudry gave a non-committal shrug. "All my father-in-law wishes is to be of service to the Marquise. And if she is pleased with that service, then he may request a favor—eventually."

"A favor with a title attached for his son—your husband— mayhap?" drawled the Duke with a raise of his black brows.

Michelle Haudry nodded, a slight flush to her cheeks. "As you are aware, M'sieur le Duc, a Farmer-General who can boast a daughter-in-law who is of the nobility is not to be scoffed at, but without the requisite entrée to court and the king, there is little prospect of the Haudry family gaining a noble title." She smiled thinly. "You are quite correct, M'sieur le Duc. It is the way of the world, for those who are used to getting what they want, that the one thing they cannot have becomes the obsession. And so it is with my father-in-law. He is established in his profession and wealthy, so what he craves now is to secure his family's future. He can do that with your help, M'sieur le Duc."

"M'sieur Haudry realises that even if I bring him to the attention of the King or his mistress, there is no guarantee either will take to him, or do him any favors."

"He is willing to take that risk, M'sieur le Duc." A light came to Michelle Haudry's dark eyes, and she smiled crookedly when she added, "But as he is arrogantly charming, I have every confidence he will achieve his object with Mme la Marquise de Pompadour, if given the opportunity. If you will pardon me offering a compliment, for I mean no disrespect when I say that you and he are alike in this regard."

Antonia leaned into the Duke and smiled up at him with a twinkle. "I would like to meet M'sieur Haudry."

"I do not doubt that he desires to make your acquaintance also, *ma vie*," the Duke replied softly, unconsciously leaning in to her. But he quickly brought himself up short, for he had been a mere moment away from kissing her in public. He sat back and turned to a footman to order a second dish of coffee.

Michelle Haudry mentally sighed, witnessing the moment and wishing her husband looked at her the way this duke looked at his duchess. But she shook herself free of such frivolous thoughts because she had a task to perform and her father-in-law was relying on her, as was her sister. Yet, she was distracted enough that she caught only the end of the Duke's question, and her faraway expression forced him to repeat it.

"And for this small favor of an introduction, what does M'sieur Haudry offer in return?"

TWENTY-SIX

F OLLOWING THE Duke's lead, Michelle Haudry came straight to the point.

"M'sieur le Duc, my father-in-law is aware of the delicate balance which exists between you and your Salvan relatives. It is on the public record the *lettre de cachet* that had the Comte de Salvan banished to his estate was at your instigation. With banishment came the loss of his court preferments. As a consequence, his family has suffered financial hardship…"

Pausing to swallow, throat parched and lips dry, she wished she had accepted the second dish of coffee. What had brought on this sudden dryness was the remarkable transformation of the Duke at her mention of the *lettre de cachet*. His features hardened. Softness and light vanished from his eyes. In their place was an implacability to the angular features which told her all she needed to know, and what she would convey to her father-in-law, without the need to ask the Duke directly: The Comte de Salvan would never be forgiven by M'sieur le Duc de Roxton; thus there was no possibility of him receiving a pardon from the king, and so there was no hope of his rehabilitation to Society.

Knowing this meant that the offer she would make on behalf of her father-in-law—as they had discussed before her visit—had to be most generous. M'sieur Haudry was prepared to give almost everything for the Duke to bestir himself for an introduction to the King's mistress, and in turn to the King himself. Yet she was acutely aware her host was under no obligation. And if he did not bestir himself, then all hopes of M'sieur Haudry's son—her husband—ever becoming ennobled, and thus the family being uplifted into the noble stratosphere were at an end. As daughter of a duke, she was less troubled by this consequence than she was the uncertain fate of her sister and the future Elisabeth-Louise hoped to have with the Chevalier Montbelliard, if the Duke proved implacable. Their fates rested with her powers of persuasion.

"Madame, all this, as you have needlessly pointed out, is known," the Duke stated flatly, breaking into her mental musings. "If you would get to the point."

"Of course, M'sieur le Duc," Michelle Haudry replied quietly, gaze bravely flickering up to the Duke's dark eyes. "Society may believe that you had the Comte de Salvan served with a *lettre de cachet* to have him out of the way so you could elope with Mme la Duchesse, but my father-in-law is in possession of the facts. That the Comte's mad son attacked the Duchess when she was with child and—"

"No! No! Not another word! I have heard enough!"

It was Antonia, and she was up off the chaise, hands clasped tightly together at her breasts. The Duke was instantly on his feet. So too was Michelle Haudry, face white and gaze cast to the carpet, unable to articulate her mortification for upsetting the couple, particularly the Duchess whose distress was writ across her beautiful face.

The Duke jerked his head at a footman, signal to escort their guest out.

"This interview is at an end, madame."

"Wait," Antonia countered, and when Michelle Haudry turned

back she looked up at the Duke, and whispered, after shuddering in a breath, "I—I am sorry. I did not mean to be foolish, but it cannot be helped. I do not wish to re-live that episode, Renard. I cannot. But we must hear what Madame Haudry has to say."

The Duke covered her clasped hands with his and lightly touched his forehead to hers.

"There is nothing for which you need apologise, *ma belle*. We are of the same mind. You have always said, have you not, that we must look to the future. As for this interview, we are under no obligation to anyone. And I won't have you upset." He gently kissed her temple. "I have finished my correspondence for the day, so let us visit the Gallery and our son before Vallentine overwhelms us with trims and drapery choices."

"I would like nothing better, Monseigneur, but I want to help this young couple. The Chevalier he did not ask to be Salvan's heir, and he surely does not wish to be your enemy. Did he not prove that his allegiance is to you and not the Salvans, with his forewarning at the inn about *Tante Philippe*'s scheming? I understand you cannot do anything that is counter to your honor, nor should you, and I do not want to put you in an impossible position. But just like our son, Elisabeth-Louise's child deserves to have a father, and a home, and a future, *hein*?" She smiled up at him brightly. "If anyone can find a way out of this quandary, it is you."

Her dazzling smile full of hope and optimism never failed to weaken his resolve. But it was her unswerving belief in him that was his undoing. How could he refuse her? He certainly did not want to disappoint her. He threw up a hand in capitulation.

"Is that what M'sieur Haudry is offering, madame?" the Duke asked, turning to look at his guest. "A future for the young couple? That is the Duchess's wish. If your father-in-law can provide that, then we can resume this conversation. If not…"

"As it so happens, that is precisely what he is offering, M'sieur le Duc et Mme la Duchesse," Michelle Haudry replied demurely, looking from one to the other.

"Then please sit, Mme Haudry," Antonia stated buoyantly, and resumed her seat on the upholstered chaise with hands clasped in her lap, the Duke sitting beside her. "And tell us all about M'sieur Haudry's proposal!"

Michelle Haudry did as instructed, took a deep breath, and addressed the couple.

"My father-in-law wishes to assure you, M'sieur le Duc, that he is mindful of the delicate balance which exists between you and your Salvan relatives. He also understands that the Chevalier Montbelliard finds himself in an awkward position, because of the circumstance of birth. As heir to the Comte de Salvan, he has unwittingly become your enemy. I do not think you wish the young man ill, but your honor will not permit you to go back on your word to disavow the Salvan line. The neatest solution would be for the Chevalier to simply go away and leave you and your family in peace. But how can he do that when he is championed by your aunts, and the rest of the Salvan family? And to complicate matters further he wishes to marry my sister, daughter of one of your closest friends."

"I wondered when you would come to the crux of the matter, madame," the Duke drawled. "Let me guess! You are about to divulge that your father-in-law is a conjuror and with his tricks can make Montbelliard disappear? Better still, the entire Salvan miscellany!"

Michelle Haudry blushed. "Something like that, M'sieur le Duc."

Antonia sat forward, fascinated. "Oh? I would like to see this trick very much!"

"What Madame Haudry's father-in-law is offering is to have Montbelliard disappear from Society altogether, *mignonne*," the Duke explained gently.

Antonia frowned. "But—he can bring him back again, from wherever he sends him, *hein?*"

"If I may be so bold, Mme la Duchesse…?" When Antonia

nodded, Michelle Haudry continued. "My father-in-law may indeed effect the Chevalier's disappearance, but only M'sieur le Duc has the power to grant his return." She inclined her head to the Duke. "If having him return is your wish…"

The Duke sat back and polished his quizzing glass with a knowing smile, while the Duchess looked from their guest to her husband, digesting this, then exclaimed.

"Aha! I see now how it is. You are both conjurors! You and M'sieur Haudry!" She touched the Duke's arm, eyes bright. "And that is as it should be." She turned to Michelle Haudry. "Please explain to us how this conjuring works."

"Put simply, the Chevalier will marry my sister in a quiet ceremony here at Versailles and then they will leave for an extended stay in the country."

The Duke lifted an eyebrow. "How—er—extended?"

"Again, that will depend on you, M'sieur le Duc. My father-in-law will purchase a small estate for the couple, and will pay for its upkeep and their living far into the future. In return, the Chevalier will give an undertaking that neither he nor his wife nor his heirs will enter society or visit Paris or Versailles, until such time as he has your blessing to do so. Be this before or after he inherits the title. And as he holds you in great esteem, and aims to please you, I have no doubts he will swear an oath never to go near, or have any correspondence with, the Comte de Salvan."

"Does M'sieur Haudry have a particular estate in mind?" enquired the Duke.

"A small chateau overlooking the Rhône, with a considerable vineyard attached. It was built at the turn of this century for an archbishop. My father-in-law's acquisition of the property will ease the considerable financial burden on the priest's family—"

"Then everyone is satisfied!" Antonia announced. "You mentioned the River Rhône, but where in particular, for it has its beginning in the Swiss Alps and empties into the Mediterranean.

But as the chateau is surrounded by vineyards, I presume it is somewhere in the south, yes?"

"Why, yes, Mme la Duchesse, it is," Michelle Haudry replied, impressed by Antonia's knowledge of geography. "The closest town is Arles—"

"Oh! How lucky is your sister and the Chevalier!" Antonia declared. "There is so much to explore in Arles, for it was once an important port for the Romans. But you probably knew that," she said to the Duke, before addressing their guest. "There are the most wonderous ruins, with much of the amphitheatre still standing, and so too the circus. And there are the remains of an aqueduct, and-and flour mills! Constantine he had baths built there, too."

"I wish Vallentine had shown half your enthusiasm for the remnants of antiquity when he and I were on the Grand Tour," the Duke quipped with an unconscious grin for her unbridled enthusiasm. "Better still, that you had been with me. When did you visit Arles, *ma fée?*"

"*Mon père* and I we stayed only a few days. We were on our way to Genoa, and taking the coast road." She sighed her disappointment. "Sadly, we did not have the time to see all that we hoped." She leaned into him and asked breathlessly, "Mayhap we could visit Arles one day."

"I would like that very much."

"Bon! Then it is settled!"

They exchanged a loving smile, and for a few moments they were the only two in the room. It was Antonia who moved time on when she turned to Michelle Haudry and asked,

"Your sister she would be content as the wife of a provincial gentleman? Is she aware Arles is far from the court and Paris and her family, that she might as well be living in St. Petersburg?"

"Mme la Duchesse, I am ashamed to admit that I had less sympathy for my sister's predicament than did my father-in-law. Elisabeth-Louise has, as they say, made her bed. If she were now commanded to live in St. Petersburg then so be it. As the Chevalier's wife she must do what is in his best interests, and the interests of their child." She smiled and unwittingly a note of tenderness crept into her voice when she admitted, "But my father-in-law is a gentleman of great sensitivity. He did not want the couple to suffer unduly, and so he chose the estate on the outskirts of Arles because Montbelliard's sister is married to a local official—I believe he has something to do with the shipment of cargo up and down the river. No matter. What is important is that they will have family close by." She addressed the Duke. "And Arles is far enough away that I doubt any member of the Salvan family will ever interfere in their lives again. So, as you rightly suggested, Mme la Duchesse, they might as well be living in St. Petersburg."

"M'sieur Haudry is indeed a conjuror, and everything it arranges itself," Antonia replied happily, and looked to the Duke. "You are satisfied with these arrangements, Monseigneur?"

"I am, *mignonne*," he responded, pocketing his quizzing glass and addressing their guest. "Madame, you may offer up my congratulations to M'sieur Haudry on his ingenuity in finding a solution to a situation that was fast becoming a problem. You may also tell him that when next I am in company with Madame la Marquise de Pompadour—which will be in a few days' time—I will be sure to whisper his good name in her ear."

"Thank you, M'sieur le Duc. I cannot wait to share the good news with my father-in-law—"

"So he can stop wearing your carpet to threads, yes?" Antonia said with a smile, as she stood, the Duke and Madame Haudry doing likewise. But instead of bringing the interview to a close, she said with a perspicacity for another's sentiments that never failed to surprise the Duke, "I see why M'sieur le Duc your father he values your opinion. But it is your father-in-law who appreciates your brain better than anyone else in your family or his. You appreciate each other."

Michelle Haudry was instantly flustered by the Duchess's

insightfulness, but she managed to answer in a steady voice. "We do, Mme la Duchesse. And if I am able to help him achieve his ambition for his family, most particularly for my husband and our children, then I am not unhappy."

"Perhaps there are other ways in which you may be of assistance to your father-in-law's ambition," the Duke said thoughtfully. "One that permits you to put to good use your brain and wise counsel. But we will talk of that on another day, and with M'sieur Haudry present. Now it is time for you to give him the good news, and we are wanted elsewhere."

Michelle Haudry bobbed a curtsey, admitting with a small smile, "As you have placed your faith in me, I wish to be entirely open with you, M'sieur le Duc et Mme la Duchesse. I was the one who persuaded my father-in-law to allow me to broker this deal on his behalf. That as the daughter of one of your closest friends, I would be more acceptable to you, than the entreaties of a Farmer-General. But my motives were not entirely selfless."

"Let me guess," Roxton drawled. "You had to see for yourself if the whispers were true."

Antonia was mystified.

Michelle Haudry was not.

The Duke enlightened them both.

TWENTY-SEVEN

"You asked to be your father-in-law's emissary, not only to help your sister and negotiate this agreement," explained the Duke, "but so you can report back to your father about my marriage."

"Yes, M'sieur le Duc," Michelle Haudry confessed, adding in a rush, "But his happiness and best wishes for *your* happiness were entirely sincere!"

"I do not doubt that," replied the Duke. "Your father is a dear and trusted friend." He smiled crookedly. "It may surprise you to learn that he also sent you to me so I could then report back to him about *you*—"

"*Me?*" Michelle Haudry was so shocked she was uncustomarily blunt. "Why would he do that?"

"When he knew I was in need of a noblewoman to place at court whom I could implicitly trust he recommended you. He was laudatory, not as a fawning papa, but as one knowing my exacting requirements, in particular that you are thoroughly trustworthy and impervious to flattery. Is that a fair estimation, Mme Haudry?"

"It is, M'sieur le Duc, and I am."

"*Merveilleux*! However, you will need to learn to stifle your—er—surprise; Versailles is, after all, about artifice. But that can be worked on. In every other respect I believe—and I am certain the Duchess agrees with me—you are ideal."

"Thank you, M'sieur le Duc," Michelle Haudry responded and bobbed a curtsey. "I look forward to our next meeting with M'sieur Haudry present, so you can inform us both what it is you wish me to do for you."

The Duke inclined his head. "And there is the perfect response! *Touché*!"

Antonia cocked her head in thought. "As M'sieur le Duc was good enough to be honest with you, perhaps you will tell us what it is your father wishes to know in particular about our marriage."

"If I may answer that…?"

"Oh! I should have thought to ask you, Monseigneur! Of course *you* know, do you not?"

"Alphonse wishes to gloat. Like the vast majority of society, he never expected that I would marry for love."

"That is because M'sieur le Duc du Touraine he does not know *me*," Antonia announced with a beaming smile. "And when he does, he will see the truth for himself."

"He will indeed, *ma fée*. But I do believe that now Mme Haudry has spent time in our company, she has reached the same conclusion that others who know us do: Ours is a marriage not only of hearts but of minds, irrespective of the age—er—disparity."

Antonia took a deep breath and tempered her annoyance.

"Please, Monseigneur, do not bring up that great piece of nonsense ever again. I am very sure Mme Haudry she did not even notice!"

"Mignonne, if I am not mistaken, I think you will find that Mme Haudry notices *everything*. And the reason she was eager to see us for herself was precisely because of that great piece of nonsense."

"Truly?" exclaimed Antonia, turning round eyes on their guest. "But I thought you quick of brain! Surely you understand that the heart is a most determined organ and will brook no impediment when it has found love. *True love has no age—*

"*—and knows no death*," Michelle Haudry completed the saying with a sad smile. "Yes, Mme la Duchesse, I understand that now. But ten years ago, I did not. Please, do not think me unhappy. My husband is a good man, and I am a faithful wife in every way, even if my heart belongs to another. God willing, I will next have a son, and if my father-in-law's ambition for a noble lineage is realised, that is more than enough to make our family content."

Their guest had barely been shown out of the library when Antonia turned to the Duke to be gathered into his embrace. She tilted her chin up. "She will make you an excellent spy, Monseigneur! She is good at other languages, sensible, wise, and in need of feeding her brain. And you said yourself—she notices *everything. C'est fait!*"

The Duke chuckled. "Sending me reports in English on the machinations at Louis' court is hardly fit food for a keen intelligence, *mignonne*, but it will cure her boredom and give her something to do."

"And she will do it, too, because it will help M'sieur Haudry's family ambition." She frowned. "Renard, how old was she when she was married to M'sieur Haudry's son?"

"Touraine married her off several months before her fourteenth birthday. I believe her husband was a year older—"

"Just children."

"Yes. But such marriages are commonplace amongst the nobility here in France."

Antonia caught at his hand and held his gaze. "A girl of fourteen who has lived her life shut up in a convent, away from the wider world, is vastly different to a girl of eighteen who grew up with a father who let her see, read, and learn what she pleased."

He pressed his lips to the back of her hand. "I know that, *ma vie*. And every day I am thankful to him for raising you as the son he never had. I do not have one regret in marrying you, and never will. You once said that you believed we were fated to be together, and I agree with you. I would not change a thing." He smiled crookedly. "Ah, there is one thing I would change—"

"You would have married me sooner!" Antonia declared happily, snuggling into his embrace, head on his chest.

"Married you sooner," he murmured, chin resting gently on the top of her braids, "and then absconded with you to the Swiss Alps—"

Antonia pulled a little away so she could see his expression. "Swiss Alps? *Pourquoi*?"

"It is the only place I can think of where we might have had a chance of spending an entire day uninterrupted," he remarked, letting her go and looking over her fair hair to the open door. "Don't tell me," he drawled, as Lord Vallentine and Martin Ellicott strode into the room unannounced. "You've come to a vital decision?"

Vallentine stuck up both hands from which dangled colorful sheets of wallpaper and swatches of fabric; Martin Ellicott did likewise.

"Which do you prefer?" he asked eagerly, putting one hand forward, "The blue with the white—"

"Egyptian blue and egg-shell white," Martin Ellicott interrupted helpfully, giving the colors their proper nomenclature.

His Lordship thrust the other hand forward, "—or the pink with the yellow?"

"Rose Pink and Naples Yellow," stated Ellicott.

Vallentine jerked his head at Martin, signal for him to come forward with his choices. "Or what Ellicott has: The pink with the red—"

"Persian Earth and Dragon's Blood."

"—or the purple with the red and yellow."

"Rose Madder, Dragon's Blood, with a hint of Orpiment," Martin Ellicott stated.

Both men looked eagerly to the Duke and Duchess, still holding up their choices.

"I do like the name Dragon's Blood; it suits you, Lucian," Antonia replied. "But is that one there truly blue or is it a green? What color did you call it, Martin?"

"No! Don't you start on about what is blue and what is green, and everythin' in between!" Vallentine huffed and let his arms drop heavily. "And don't you say another word, Ellicott! Blast it! We've been at this all mornin', and Estée will be wantin' to know my choices, and I have to make a hard decision—*now*." He lifted his square chin at the Duke. "Well? What do you prefer, Roxton, eh?"

"Surely you know which one I would choose?" the Duke drawled teasingly.

"Oh no! Not you, too!" Vallentine declared hotly. "You're not gettin' off that lightly. This whole decoratin' business has given me an almighty bad head. I've stopped thinkin' altogether. My brain can't take any more of this."

Antonia was all sympathy, and touched His Lordship's silken sleeve. "You have been indoors far too long, *mon beau-frère*. You need winter air. When Julian he is out of sorts, I take him outside and soon he is calm again."

"Don't tempt me! What I wouldn't give for a bit of swordplay in the winter sun!" His Lordship's shoulders sagged. "But I can't. Not till I've finalized this wretched business."

"You may curse me for saying this," said the Duke, "but have you given any thought to what your wife will choose for her rooms, and if your choices will complement hers?"

Vallentine was thunderstruck. He had not. He threw Martin Ellicott a dark look that said "*Why didn't you think of that?*".

The Duke in turn exchanged a knowing smile with his former valet, and then he told his best friend what he wanted to hear.

"Winter sun and exercise will do us both good. Oh, and she'll choose the Rose Madder, Dragon's Blood, with the hint of—er—Orpiment…? Estée is about more not less."

His Lordship gave a huge sigh of relief. "Thank God for that!" Adding sheepishly to his offsider, "You were right, Ellicott. And I thank you for your assistance." He then snatched the wallpaper strip and fabric swatch out from the man's right hand before nodding at his left. "Now be so kind as to put that collection on Roxton's desk for safe-keepin', and the wife's perusal."

And without another word, and with Antonia and Martin watching on, Vallentine tossed the discarded wallpaper strips and fabrics into the air and strode out of the library after the Duke, eager to have his sword fetched, and get out of doors.

Explore the real people, places, objects, and
history in *Her Duke* on Pinterest.
www.pinterest.com.au/lucindabrant/roxton-foundation-series

www.ingramcontent.com/pod-product-compliance
Lightning Source LLC
Chambersburg PA
CBHW051108300726
48981CB00001B/47